BANG
BANG
BANG

A NOVEL BY
AINSLEY BURROWS

Published by

BurrowsInk
1607 East 95 Street
Brooklyn NY 11236
Phone: 3474097442
Email: ainsley.burrows@gmail.com

Copyright 2013
Ainsley Burrows
Cover Design: BurrowsInk
Photo: Dennis Manuel
Book layout BurrowsInk

Contact the author:
Facebook.com/ainsleyburrows
Twitter @ainsleyburrows
Instagram @ainsleyburrows

published 2013.

Dedication

This book is dedicated to Brooklyn and all the beautiful people who make Brooklyn magical.

Special Thanks

Laurielle Noel
Henry Richards
Kalita Cox
Venny Rose
Tameka Feaster
Janine Breland

Bang Bang **BANG**

BurrowsInk

Chapter One

He never thought in a million years this could ever happen to him. How did he get to this point? His brain was racing. It was sad really. Here he was, a high powered lawyer, with a knife shoved up under his chin. He could feel the steel pushing forcefully into his flesh.

"Listen, babe," he could barely squeeze the words out. "I don't know what you're talking about."

"Shut the fuck up Max," she said with her eyes filled with tears, her hand shaking like a leaf.

There they were, a beautiful couple, in their sprawling Clinton Hill apartment with a view to die for, and what were they doing? She was getting ready to murder him.

She shoved the knife harder. "Don't lie to me Max. All I want you to do is tell me the truth; the truth Max, the fucking truth!"

Her lips were quivering. She was straddled over him. He could feel the warmth of her crotch against him.

"What truth are you talking about?"

"Max you know what I'm talking about, motherfuckin' Vanessa, Max!"

"Vanessa? What, what are you talking about?"

"Did you fuck her Max?" She jammed the knife a little harder and crinkled her face.

Max let out a small plea. "Babe stop."

"Did you fuck her?"

Max moved his eyes to the side and strained under the pressure of the knife. He saw his cell phone right next to his wrist watch and his keys on the side table. There was a text on the screen, and last night flew through his head in a flash.

He was sitting at the Brooklyn Moon. It was supposed to be just a regular after work meet-up to grab a glass of wine or a beer. He had not seen Vanessa in a few months.

Max was there first, he sat facing the door, not because he was sitting by himself but more so because he wanted to watch the women as they passed. He had a problem with avoiding looking at women's asses, and the stretch of Fulton Street between Lafayette and Green Avenues was notorious for having some of the most perfect backsides in all of Brooklyn. The summer was ripe and so were the women who wore as little as they could.

A small speaker on the floor pumped music into the room. Max was in a zone. Something about this place just said sexy; the sun, the smells coming from the kitchen, all the couples sitting across from each other and looking into each other's eyes. *"This is beautiful,"* Max thought to himself. Why didn't he and his fiancé have this?

The reflection of the sun came through the trees that were across the street and for a moment Max was struck blind. He felt the knife pushing harder into his chin. He was back in his bed, looking up into Sophie's hazel eyes.

"Max this is the last time I'm going to ask you. Did you fuck her Max?"

She stared into his face searching for truth. He closed his eyes; and *Bang*. He was back in the Brooklyn Moon.

His vision was back and standing in the doorway like a glowing orb was Vanessa. Vanessa was the complete opposite of Sophie. She was into art and politics. She was "free" in every way imaginable. She had a head of natural hair that in and of itself was a statement to the world. Plus she was thick. Not just normal thick, but that good kind of thick that you could not resist. And most of all she was a flawless cocoa brown that Max secretly admired.

She stood in the door and waited for her eyes to adjust.

"Hey Max." She walked over.

"Hey Vanessa, look at you, Mm."

"What?" She looked him up and down.

"Looking fine as ever."

She smiled.

"Have a seat," he said quietly, "let me take a look at you."

"Stop playing, how is your fiancé?"

"She's good."

And after that statement everything seemed like a blur. It was only supposed to be drinks. After about four rounds, bouts of laughter and an accidental awkward meeting of eyes, they fell into a surreal groove. A kind of psychosexual insanity raged through them both. And *Bang*, they found themselves in the back of a yellow cab tearing the clothes off of each other.

It was not planned. It was all improv; they were like two jazz musicians tearing into unknown musical territory. And before he could think about it or she could change her mind, his dick was being sucked beautifully by a pair of what could probably be the sexiest lips in the world.

The driver kept his eye on the road as the night splashed about outside the window. His fingers dug deeper and deeper into her unshaven vagina. It was so watery he was beside himself. *"Is this even possible?"* he thought.

He had always imagined what her pussy must have felt like, but this was beyond anything he could have conjured.

He slipped his fingers into her mouth and smeared a little of the cream on her lips, she sucked on his fingers. He smiled a mischievous smile, then glided his hands back up under her flowing skirt, pulled her aggressively across the seat of the cab and planted his face fully into the sweet pleat. She gyrated against his tongue and just kept getting wetter and wetter.

"225 Macon," the cab driver said barely peering over his shoulder.

Max reached into his wallet, as Vanessa was getting herself together.

"How much?"

"Nine dollars."

He stuffed a twenty into the little money window. Vanessa stepped out of the cab, he slid out behind her, and they disappeared into her ground level brownstone apartment.

It took a few minutes to get the key into the hole, mainly because she was distracted by him on his knees behind her with his tongue pressed into her. His two palms held her pelvis in place as she spun slow circles with her waist. She got the key in and turned.

They did not even take a breath before he had her kneeling on the floor in front of her bed with one leg thrown up on the mattress and the other being eaten slowly by rug burn. Every stroke came not from some desire to have mere sex, but a desire to be so deep inside of her that his dick was numb with happiness.

She moaned and pushed back against him and he bit into her. She panted and begged him to grab her hair and for him to pull it so hard that she howled as she came and he felt her coming. The constriction of her inner flesh against his dick motivated him to no end. This was what he wanted; a woman who moaned and screamed and told him to call her a whore and demanded he fuck her harder.

He felt an erotic kind of joy pounding in his chest. Looking down on her beautiful brown body, smooth and supple, just moving in such a fluid motion made him pause.

And inside his head he said a quiet prayer, then said, "I want to fuck you like this every day. Let me fuck you like this every day."

She screamed back at him half panting, half moaning, half *thank you note*. "Yes you can fuck me like this anytime you waaaaaaant!"

She came again. And he plunged deeper into all that wetness. And *Bang*. He exploded. And a divine energy coursed through his veins.

"This-is-the-best-pus-sy-I-have-e-ver-had," he said in staccato.

And just like that he looked up at Sophie and said, "I did not fuck her, ok."

There was blood in Sophie's eyes. "You fucking liar!"

She raised the knife above her head just as the sun was about to rise, the light climbed into their spacious bedroom as she slammed the knife into his chest. Max grabbed his chest and gasped.

"Honey you ok?" Sophie reached over and passed her hand across his chest. He was dreaming again.

"That shit was too fucking real," he thought to

himself.

Sophie made a sound that he knew ever so well. She wanted to make love. They made love every morning. Like clockwork. On schedule. It was 6:35am. She was ready. She tugged at him. He climbed on top of her.

And approximately eight and a half minutes later she was saying, "I'm coming, I am coming. I. Am. Coming!"

After she came, he got a few extra strokes in and grunted and she nudged him off. Yes he came. But was he satisfied? No. All he could think about was Vanessa.

Chapter Two

Brenton is a fast talker. In another incarnation he could have been a pimp. Well at some level you can say he is a pimp. He prides himself on being able to speak for his living. He is from the Caribbean, but you would not be able to tell unless he wanted you to.

He went to Syracuse University on a full soccer scholarship; he studied marketing, and after school he went into business booking up-and-coming artists. It's been about 10 years since college and he was developing a slight belly. But his powers were still stronger than ever.

He has this thing he does, that he learned from his cousin Trace, it has never failed him. He had been doing it since he was in college. The way it worked was like this; he could point at a woman, any woman and for a period of 24 hours she would be fully under his spell if he chose. Because of this *gift*, he hung out at Habana Outpost all summer. It was kind of like shooting fish in a barrel.

"Yow, what's up?" he answered.

His phone was always ringing; one moment,

Hong Kong; the next moment London, or Philly or Miami, or Austin or Seattle or some random place in west bubble fuck USA. Every call was either money or pussy.

"Yeah, yeah, I got that for you. I'll send it over now." He clicked on an app on his phone, opened an email, hit forward and typed in an email address. He hit send.

"Just sent it." He paused and took the phone away from his ear and hit speaker.

The voice droned out. "Can you do any better than this mate?"

"Listen man, this is a fuckin' giveaway right now. Just got a call from LA who wants to book him that same week for ninety five; this is KEV we're talking about, Young Kevlar. I know you may just be trying to squeeze something off the back end for yourself, but right now this is the best we can do." All said in about five seconds.

The voice on the phone was doubtful. "Nothing you can do mate?"

This was Stuart, an old talent buyer from London. Stuart changed gears.

"Look Brenton, if you can get him to me at 70, I can get you at least 5 dates," he turned on the old English charm.

"Don't fall for it Brent," Brenton said to himself. He took a deep breath then went into crisis mode.

"Ok, check this out; when you're ready to do business, give me a call back *–OK mate*," Brenton said in his best English accent and hung up.

He then sat his phone down on the table in front of him and took a sip from his coffee. He eyed a redhead sitting by herself on the other side of the courtyard. She smiled at him. He pointed at his phone and mouthed something to her. She squinted trying to read his lips. He had already decided she was his. She just didn't know it yet.

She had Hamptons hair and was a little nerdy; not totally off the deep end nerd, kind of nerd chic. She was probably writing a screenplay or a sitcom about New York socialites or something. His phone rang. He smiled, it was Stuart. He knew his work for the day was done. He picked up and hit speaker.

The voice on the other side of the Atlantic screeched. "We'll do it mate."

"Bet, I'll send the contract over. I need it signed as soon as possible. This guy is hot right now and offers are coming in all the time. And since you are only offering seventy five..." This was too easy.

The voice jumped back in. "I'll have the contract signed and back to you by 5pm my time."

Brenton checked his watch and smiled again, he knew that by 12 noon he would have the contract and a down payment. Stuart was that kind of guy.

Brenton was a fast talker. In another life he could have been a politician or an auctioneer.

He turned back to his present target; the redhead. He pointed his finger at her and *Bang*. Something happened. Sometimes he did not even know how it happened.

She shifted in her seat and exposed her neck and gently slid her fingers through her hair. He saw the subtle exposure. He took a final sip from his coffee.

"Waiter," he called out and a young man scurried toward his table.

"How much?"

"$2.50."

Brenton already knew but he asked anyway, how else was he going to make his point?

"Cool." He slapped a twenty down on the table and moved toward the white girl.

"I'm Brenton."

They shook hands and within five minutes they were both laughing and talking like old friends. Then the obvious questions came.

"You live around here?"

"Yes."

"Get out, really, where?" he said with incredulity.

"Yeah, I live right on Lafayette in number 99. It's right on the corner, the big building…"

He interrupted her with a smile. "I know; I've been in that building a few times."

Maybe it was the way he said it, maybe it was the way she heard it, maybe it was the fact that it was 10:15 in the morning, maybe it was the gentle summer wind and the birds chirping. Whatever it was, somehow, her eyes dilated. And *Bang*; he had her deep in the back of number 99 on the 7th floor, Apt 7F. Her screenplay paused midsentence, her summer dress flung up over her tender ass as he pounded out the rest of their introduction.

"Oh-my-fuh-cking-god, I-can't-be-lieve-this-is-ha-ppen-ning, I- fuh-kin-love-your cock!" she said in her best nerd voice, her freckled breast pressed against the back window.

Brenton was knee deep in her.

"Hold on, hold on, hold on," she begged, "I can't come like this."

She reached back and eased his dick out of her slowly, turned around and looked at it with glee before devouring it. The slurping sound was like music to Brenton's ears. She looked up at him, he held her hair back.

She shoved him onto a single seat leather chair which was next to her bed and rode him to the sound of the city outside of her window.

About an hour later they both laid spent on her Ikea sheets, they had fucked three times. Her body was beautiful, soft and toned, all a nice summer copper except for her breast and bikini area. Brenton laughed to himself. Her hair was everywhere. A thin film of sweat covered them both, their chests still heaving.

Brenton thought to himself. *"Shit, what was her name again?"*

He went back to the moment they shook hands. He had said, *"I'm Brenton,"* and she had said,

nothing, just a, *"hey how are you?"* Not that he
was sad about it, but he had just nutted in this girl's
mouth and he did not even know her name.

His phone rang. He reached over her into the
pocket of his pants on the floor. It was his boy
Max. He decided not to take the call because
what's her name seemed like she needed a little
more of his attention.

Chapter Three

"Yow Max what's up?"

"Nothing, just taking it easy."

"I saw I had a missed call from you, what's poppin' tonight?"

"I was thinking about going to Vodou; just waiting for Sophie to get here. I think she is out with her girl Meghan."

"Meghan, Meghan, oh yeah that's that half Black, half Asian chick right?"

"Yeah."

"She fuckin' hates me dude."

"Why, what happened?"

"I can't even get into it."

"Come on man, you are always holding out on the details."

"Nah, it's fucking crazy."

"Come on man, wha' happened? This is me!"

"Shit… You can't tell anybody though."

"Come on Brenton, you don't even have to tell me that, I'm a lawyer, totally confidential."

"Cool, cool. Remember fourth of July when you

had that party at your crib?"

"Yeah."

"You know ever since I met Meghan she was always flirting with me right?"

"Yeah, but she flirts with everyone!"

"And you know I don't really mess with chicks that are too close to folks I know. That's Sophie's friend so for a while I was kinda trying not to fuck with her girl, but that night when she showed up in those tight ass jeans... I was like, if this bitch fuckin' slip, I'm fucking the shit outta her." His Caribbean accent came out.

Max started laughing. He knew how notorious Brenton was. If picking up women was an art, Brenton by far was the master. He had known Brenton since they were at Syracuse. He had seen this man do things that were not supposed to be humanly possible.

Once, at school, at a sorority party, by some weird magic or voodoo or whatever it was that Brenton had; Brenton convinced ten girls to take off their tops and he ranked them in order of who he thought had the most beautiful breasts. And it wasn't like he did it because he wanted to see their breasts; he did it because he thought it was fun. Fun. Brenton traded in fun.

He was always holding court; he was always the center of attention. He had this intangible thing that made people want to hear what he had to say. Max had always thought Brenton should have been a lawyer, but Brenton wanted none of it. *Fuck being a lawyer.*

"So, remember when that girl came with the weed brownies, it was probably like two in the morning?"

"There were weed brownies at the party that night?"

"What, you didn't have any?"

"Nah, you know what – I think that's when Sophie was acting weird, so we were in the bedroom talking."

"Dude your girl is always fucking buggin' bro."

"Tell me about it, she thought I was trying to have sex with Amanda. I was like Amanda is my best friend's wife, why would I try to fuck her? I think she's trying to sabotage our relationship!"

"I don't want to be the bearer of bad news, but she's crazy. I don't even know why you're engaged, but that's your fiancé so… "

"I know, I know."

They were both quiet for a while, and then Brenton chimed back in.

"So we were drinking and then had some brownies right, and she just kept flirting with me! And I'm trying my best to be a good citizen and shit and in the back of my mind I'm thinking, *'that's Sophie's friend, if I fuck her shit is bound to get ugly.'*"

Max was dying laughing on the other end of the phone.

"But this bitch is really coming at me! I ain't go'

lie, I was flirting with her too, but when the brownie kicked in... dude you don't even want to know."

"What happened, what happened?"

"You know that door by the elevators that leads to the stairwell?"

"Oh, no way. What!"

"Yep, fucked her in the stairwell, but that's not the crazy part. When I say the shit was insane, I mean in-fuckin-sane! When we were done I was buzzing so I was like – fuck it, I'ma walk her home."

"Where does she live?"

"She lives like on Classon and St. Marks or Dean, one of them streets, I don't really remember. It was a long walk, but because I was drunk that shit was kinda all blurry... We get to her crib right, and we in her room, and I'm in it, and I'm tearing it up, and she's like *stop*, *stop* because her stomach is queasy from the brownies. So she goes into the bathroom and starts throwing up. I want to go help her but I am so friggin high... I had like ten drinks that night plus the brownies. I was done right.

I'm trying to get to the bathroom and end up sitting on her couch butt naked and who walks through the door? This fly ass half-drunk chick! And I'm thinking, *'...Is that Meghan?'* I am totally naked on the couch right and this chick comes in and is like, 'wow, is that for me?' I was like, 'it could be...' And, before I could say another word, she was on my lap! She didn't even take her clothes off, she just slid her panties to the side, stuffed me in, and was riding the fuck out of me for like, I don't even know how long. Next thing I know, fucking Meghan is shouting all kinds of shit and chucking the girl off my dick!"

"Who was the chick?" Max was dying laughing.

"Turns out it was Meghan's younger sister who was visiting her from college."

"Dude you are crazy man, fuckin' craaaaaaazy!"

"So the next day she calls me up making a fuss. All I could say was I was drunk, but I think she was mostly mad because her sister had done something like that before; maybe slept with her boyfriend or something – I don't know."

"You fucked Meghan and her sister in the same night!"

"It was totally by accident though! It's not like I planned the shit, the shit just happened man."

"So you think she told Sophie?"

"I hope she didn't."

Chapter Four

The sun lit the sky from below the horizon and the oranges and purples turned Brooklyn into a giant dream. Sophie and Meghan were sitting in the back garden of Outpost.

Outpost is a kind of artsy café on Fulton. It is always fully occupied, all hours of the day and night, by pretentious, wanna be writers. If you have a screen play that is never going to sell, this is where you come to not write it. If you have a brilliant idea for a business that would never be realized, this was your place. Got a novel you've been working on for the past ten years, this is your place to not get it done. All the people with no future in art came here.

Not only was it a vacuum that swallowed up talent, it was the heart of all things futureless. They mostly played music of obscure or failed indie artists, with zero futures, who were always whining about this or that. The art on the walls was shit. Not literal shit, even though it could have been on many occasions. This place was so bad that even the servers had loser shoulders. But somehow the confluence of all these forces made it a *pretty cool* place to hang. At least everyone there was beautiful, in their own way.

Sophie looked worried.

"So what's going on?" her best friend asked.

"I don't even know where to start."

"Start from the beginning."

"We've been engaged for *two* years now Meg."

"It's been that long?"

"Yes, it's two years in September."

"A lot of people take some time to get married after they get engaged."

"Yeah, I know, but that's usually because of money."

"True, you have a point."

"Plus my dad said he would pay for the whole thing. He's already mad that we're living together, all he wants us to do is get married already."

"What do you think the problem is?"

"I don't know."

They were on their third glass of wine, you could tell by the look in their eyes. These were two beautiful women; and the warm light from the sky and the lanterns in the garden just served to illustrate that point even more.

"I don't know Meg; I think maybe we're not for each other. It's more than just the whole engagement thing." Sophie leaned over so that only Meg would hear. "The sex is terrible."

"Really?"

"Yes."

Meghan saw the loneliness in her eyes. "Have you thought about seeing a therapist?"

"A therapist? No, not really…" She threw away the answer as she shrugged.

The wine was doing its job.

"Where is the waiter?" Sophie said before emptying her glass. "You want another glass? … Waiter! Hey waiter!" she said spinning in every which direction.

A petite, model-looking young woman came over to the table, wearing her loser shoulders. She could not have been more than nineteen.

"Another glass of Shiraz for me, and a glass of ah, what was it again, another glass of Pinot for the lady," Sophie said intimating a semi-drunk English woman.

Meghan and Sophie laughed; the waitress smiled and walked off.

"It's kind of hard to believe the sex is terrible, you two are so sexy together."

"Listen," she slinked forward again, her thin fingers gently touching Meghan's hand as a bolt of current shot through Meghan's body. "We've been having sex for what, ten years? There's nothing new we can do."

"Has it always been terrible?"

"No."

"So, what do you think happened?"

"You want the truth?"

"Yeah. What do you think happened?"

"I think he's fucking somebody else, I think he's fucking Amanda," Sophie said in a whisper.

"What?" Meghan inquired, even though she heard Sophie loud and clear.

"Either that or I'm just crazy."

"Amanda. Really. Isn't that what's his name, ah Maurice's wife? ... Cheating is one thing but fucking his best friend's wife, that's a whole different story."

Sophie's face got sad. Meghan saw her sadness.

"How do you know though?"

"I saw her looking at him one day and the look wasn't the normal oh, let me check out Max, it was a *knowing* look; and right there I was like *that dirty little bitch.*"

"Do you have any evidence?"

"Evidence? No. But..."

"You sure you're not just paranoid?"

"No, this is not paranoia. I know what I saw. She was eye fucking my man," Sophie shot her a stern look.

"Eye fucking someone does not mean anything Sophie."

"Yes it does!" her words slurred.

"I have to go to the bathroom." Meghan used the statement to clear the air.

"Me too."

They both tramped off to the single occupant bathroom. It was a tight space. Meghan squatted over the toilet as Sophie fixed her almost non-existent lips in the mirror above the sink.

"You think I'm beautiful Meg?"

This was a strange question for Meg to answer because, well it's a long story, but needless to say she thought the world of Sophie.

"Of course, are you kidding me, you are maybe the most beautiful woman I know."

"Really? Thank you so much," Sophie said looking at her drunk self in the mirror.

Meg was washing her hands. "You know you're beautiful right?"

Sophie was silent for a few seconds. "Sometimes I don't feel like it."

Meg's heart broke inside her chest. She hit the drier with the back of her hand. The breeze shot through her fingers and up under her skirt; and the buzzing sound; and the sweet smell of the hand soap; and her heart breaking; and Sophie's sadness; and the alcohol walking through her veins all collided, and for no given reason – *Bang*.

Meg turned around and planted a kiss flush on Sophie's mouth. Sophie had a sweet mouth, and the taste of the wine made it even sweeter. Meghan had experimented with women in college and every now and then she might have an encounter with a woman. She never considered herself gay or even bi. It was just something that she did.

Sophie, on the other hand, was pretty straight-laced. This was completely outside of her worldview, but for some reason she was totally turned on. Maybe it was the passion with which Meghan slipped her tongue into her mouth, the softness of her lips, her firm breasts pressed against hers, the gentle way Meg's hands slowly slipped down to her backside. Sophie let out a gasp. Lost her breath; she could barely speak.

"Oh my God, what are we doing?"

She wanted to stop her best friend Meghan – what were they doing? But it felt so good, so fucking good to be wanted this badly. A tear came to her eye. This is how she wanted Max to want her.

"I've wanted to do this for so long Sophie," Meghan mumbled with her mouth full of lips.

Meghan's hands were in places and touching things in ways that two really, really good friends should not be touching each other. Sophie was lost in the passion and just went along, she just said fuck it and let go. She was open to being totally consumed, to being devoured, to being wanted this bad. This kind of passion was like a miracle at this moment.

Meghan had one of Sophie's nipples in her mouth and two fingers inside of her in one moment, and in the next moment all Sophie knew was she was sitting on the toilet top spread eagle and Meghan was passionately eating her pussy with such meticulous fervor that she did not know what to say or do. Involuntarily some words stumbled out of her mouth.

"Why, why Meghan, why are you eating my pussy this good?" She started tearing up again.

Meghan's fingers were hitting her g-spot and Sophie could feel the room tightening around her. She had not been in this place in years. All those *"I am coming, I am coming,"* she did when she had sex with Max, chalk that up to the work she did as a theater major at Clark Atlanta University.

Meghan could feel Sophie tightening around her fingers; and feel her thighs squeezing against her head. Sophie arched her back and let out an inaudible scream. And in the most vulnerable moment in her life she squirted all over Meghan's face. Meghan was fully alive; she was her most alive watching this, her best friend having what may have been her first experience squirting. Meghan licked her lips and smiled. Life was beautiful.

Chapter Five

Maurice and Amanda were a perfect couple. They had a daughter who was turning eleven. Maurice was from a southern family, in South Carolina. Where they came from, his family had a name. He was like royalty in Charleston.

At twenty-two he married a freshman student. He had gotten her pregnant, so he did what a southern man does. She dropped out to have the baby and he stayed on and finished up his senior year. After school, she was a stay-at-home mom, which at the time was fine but now her daughter was almost a teen and she had spent most of her twenties being a mother and going to school part time.

All those years Maurice lived a completely different life than his wife. He was in finance, which meant the money was good, very good. His family was well taken care of, but he was almost never around.

Amanda, on the other hand, was totally committed to their marriage. When Maurice was not home she spent most of her time reading erotic novels. She was addicted, saying she needed rehab was an understatement.

Maurice and his boys were always all over the country blowing off steam, had something to do with the stress levels of his job. Maurice must have been away about 25 weekends out of every year and in all that time he had been unfaithful, sometimes he had different women, sometimes it would be a repeat affair.

His crew or his band of conspirators, Milton, Brovec, Muhammed and Oluyemisi got themselves a four bedroom suite at Trump Soho to celebrate Brovec's birthday. They were a strange group, mainly because of their genetic make-up. Beyond that, they were like quintuplets, they walked the same, talked the same, and dressed the same.

Everything they did was about flash. Milton was Jewish, non-practicing, and graduated from Wharton. Muhammed, Indian American background, Columbia graduate, math. Brovec was from Kiev, graduated from MIT, masters in statistics. Oluyemisi was recruited because of his work in systems engineering. He was by far the most brilliant of the group. And Maurice graduated from Syracuse, business law, then got his MBA at Harvard Business School. They were all young, moneyed, and filled with testosterone.

Since it was Brovec's birthday weekend, he wanted to go to Vegas, but as a group they decided to stay in New York City. Fuck Vegas, New York was the capitol of the world.

That night they did a club run. Maurice had a friend Brenton he knew from college. He and Max had helped Brenton set up his artist booking agency. Brenton knew all the best clubs in NYC and most of all, knew how to get them in the door, with bottle service etc.

It was never about the money for these guys, it was all about how it looked. To get into some of these clubs was probably about twenty or thirty dollars on most nights. A good top shelf drink was about twenty five bucks. But to walk up to a club with a line around the block and just *walk in*; that was PRICELESS.

They were always going for the: *"Who the hell are those guys?"* effect.

The only rule they had for their nights out was they only did shots, only top shelf. They were like five James Bonds, going from place to place doing shots with beautiful women and snapping photos and posting them. Tonight was different; they were going shopping, shopping for beautiful women.

The sunset was beautiful on the roof of The Gansevoort. You could see entire stretches of lower Manhattan, and the Hudson River, streaked by water traffic. The guys were toasting to Brovec, first shot of the night. Oluyemisi checked his watch; it was early, 9:15pm, so they had tons of time.

They had only been there for barely fifteen minutes and Maurice had already convinced two young ladies that they were in for the night of their lives. One of the girls was a beautiful, petite black girl with a fro-hawk and a tiny button nose. Her friend was of Italian background, and looked like a taller version of Kim Kardashian. They were a fine pull. All the guys needed now were two more until the next spot.

It was 10pm on the dot; they were rolling into Buddha Bar. They were doing better numbers than expected. They had six women in their group so far. It was all hands, smiles, laughs and flirtatious banter. It's amazing what two shots of Café Patron can do for a conversation.

They moved into Buddha Bar like a den of spies. They had a few rounds, sang Happy Birthday did a group hug and then one last shot for Brovec.

Everyone was at a beautiful medium. They were in a drinker's limbo, somewhere between tipsy and barely drunk. Another four women joined their group – they were totally loving the plan.

These new girls were professional socialites. These were the type that Maurice liked. They didn't take much of what they did seriously. They did it for the fun and for the perks. A Prada bag here, a Louis V purse there, a trip to Vegas or Miami.

Not that it was a contest, but in the morning there would be stories about blow jobs in bathroom stalls, and finger popping girls in the VIP at Tenjune, what girl threw up or passed out, and how many

shots who had and who got whose number. These
nights were literally anything goes.

But tonight was special because it was a gift for
their friend Brovec. So they were all standing on
the seats in Tenjune singing at the top of their
lungs. *"Tonight, ama love love you tonight, give
me everything tonight, for all we know we might not
see tomorrow…"* And for a moment there, they
were all gay. Not gay like homosexual, but gay
like you could hug a dude during the song and it
would be ok.

Milton, Muhammad, Oluyemisi, Brovec and
Maurice had their hands in the air singing,
surrounded by sixteen beautiful girls and one
chunky chick with a whole lot of personality, all
vying for a top spot. The bottles of Grey Goose
were almost out. Everyone was filled with the
same amount of happiness. Some of the girls were
hugging. Two of the professional socialites were
making out. One of them gently took Brovec's
hand and pulled him towards them - he joined in.

Oluyemisi looked at his watch, and then around
the room after the song ended. The petite black girl
with the fro-hawk was fast asleep. Maurice had his
finger pressed into the lower back of the tall Kim
Kardashian look-a-like while another young
woman, dressed in the least amount of clothes
allowed off Staten Island, had her hands clasped
around his waist. Milton was fully engaged in a
slurry conversation about Nietzsche with the

Chunky girl; Milton had game but he was always willing to take one for the team, even when he didn't have to.

They walked into the club at Trump SoHo with their newly minted drunkenness just as the party was on the brink of winding down. They stood in the doorway, all twenty one of them like a murder of crows about to go on a feeding frenzy. When they stepped into the room they brought with them a kind of mayhem and festive chaos that reignited the party.

More drinks, more shots, more dancing, more women, more slurred speech, more kissing on the dance floor, more group hugs, more grinding, more drinks, more drinks, more drinks, more of everything. And for a moment there was no sound coming from the speakers, just the booming bass pushing against their bodies, and someone's hand was up someone's skirt. Someone else had a fist full off ass and a mouth full of tongue and a shot in the air.

"To Brovec!"

They all swallowed their drink, made that face and the room was back to normal. Bodies pushed up close against each other, all hands in the air singing and swaying.

It was now 3:45am and they stumbled into the hotel lobby with a group of about 17 girls. The rest of the night's revelry can't be put into words. There was enough alcohol, weed and coke to kill a small army, but somehow this group of crazies was still alive the next morning. The hotel suite was a total wreck. There were half naked women all over the place.

Maurice pushed Brovec's room door open.

"Dude last night was fuckin' insane!" Brovec had two girls in the bed and one sleeping on the floor.

"Dude did you fuck that fat chick?" Brovec mouthed back to Maurice in a whisper.

"No way, just got a little," he made the sign for blow job. "But Milton did."

Brovec narrowed his eyes, using some of that Soviet truth serum he learned from his grandmother.

"Ok, ok. I did too… Did you do all of them?" Maurice made a ridiculous face, his eyes bulging.

"No, just," then Brovec pointed at the girl on the floor and the one on his right.

"Damn!" Maurice was happy for him.

The two girls who were supposed to be chillin with him had gotten too high and too drunk to mess with, so he slid the fat girl from under Milton while Milton was in the bathroom getting high. She did give him some head and maybe he returned the favor, but that is a big maybe; there were a lot of drugs involved, so the story is up for review.

Maurice pushed Muhammad's room door open. His friend was dead asleep, passed out on the floor next to the bed. The four socialites were wide awake and going at it. They all paused for a moment, looked at him, they all smiled and just like that –*Bang*. Maurice entered his first five-some.

Chapter Six

Last Saturday Amanda and Max decided to meet at Oleo. Oleo is a small Italian restaurant that looks as if it was ripped out of an ancient gentile town somewhere in Italy and plopped down on the corner of Lafayette and Adelphi in Fort Greene.

It was early May and, a bit chilly, so sitting outside was not particularly attractive; aside from the obvious fact that these two should not be meeting alone. What was Max thinking meeting with his best friend's wife? What was Amanda thinking meeting with her husband's best friend?

Max was a little late. He walked in and scanned the room. A two piece duo, near the entrance, one on guitar the other on percussion, was keeping the dinners charmed with renditions of old world Italian songs. Max spotted Amanda. She waved him over. She was smiling. They hugged. Maybe it was because he was doing something so forbidden but he was fully aroused. Something about Amanda just turned him on. They sat.

"So, how are you?"

"I'm good," Amanda replied. Her eyes were

smiling; if Max did not know any better he would think she was in love.

"So, ah it's good to see you," he was a little nervous.

"Same here," she reached across the table and touched his hand softly.

"What are we going to do?" Max said as he felt her energy pass into his body.

Amanda shrugged. It was one of those I don't give a fuck shrugs. And in that moment Max knew that they would be fucking in a few hours, maybe a few minutes, maybe a few seconds.

"We should not be doing this Amanda," he tried to sound sincere.

She smiled at his attempt at being serious. She knew he wanted it as much as she did so she slid her hand under the table and reached for his thigh. They looked into each other's eyes for a few seconds. Max started sweating, he looked around the room then had a flashback to the moment he first entered her.

There was something so glorious about the way she bit into his bottom lip and pushed up towards him. They had never intended to fuck like that. It just happened. They had been circling each other for years. There had always been a little sexual tension between them but they were both in life-long relationships.

Worse even, Max and Maurice were best friends. But that evening in April when Max stopped over to see Maurice and it turned out Maurice had forgotten their meeting, Amanda decided *why not?* Why not have drinks with a friend since her husband was never around.

"Maurice said he'd be here?" Amanda asked.

"Yes he did," Max answered.

"That's strange, I spoke with him today and he said he was gonna be at the office late."

"Mm, I spoke with him today and he said he was gonna be here."

"How about *we* get a drink?" Amanda said with her head tilted to the side.

Max caught it the moment it came out her mouth. All that yearning.

"You sure?" he asked her earnestly.

"Very sure," she said in a half whisper.

"Where do you wanna go?"

"We could stay right here," the yearning in her voice surfaced again.

Max was not sure they were talking about the same thing. So he tested her with one last question.

"What kind of drink do you want?"

He knew exactly where this question would lead. Maybe he was taking advantage of her. He knew she was lonely, he knew his boy was never around. Why would he ask such a question?

Amanda smiled a coy smile, walked right up to Max and placed her lips real close to his ear and said, "I want a really stiff drink."

Max pulled back and looked her in the eyes and

quietly asked, "Really?"

Amanda slipped her hand over the front of his pants and said, "Yes, really."

She felt his dick rising in her palm; she stroked it a few times. He grabbed her ass. She let out a soft sigh. He was rock hard by now. She slowly unzipped his pants and slipped her hand through the zipper and into his boxer briefs. His dick was warm. He cupped her ass even harder. She looked at him and licked her lips a little. They kissed, and God it was scary and it was good. She stroked his dick while they kissed. He used his teeth to pull her strapless top down; her breasts were a sight to behold. She had thick dark nipples. He thought about Maurice.

Why was he doing this to Maurice's wife? *"Stop Max!"* he kept saying to himself. As he was about to get a mouthful of her breast, she flicked his dick out of his pants and got on her knees. If there was a way out, God knows it just closed.

He closed his eyes in anticipation. She slowly licked the tip.

"Oh my God," Max let out.

She continued, slowly and gently. This was not a blow job. This was closer to worship. She undid his belt. She had never been with another man before. She had always fantasized about what it would feel like. She paused for a moment and inhaled deeply. She looked up at Max. Max's eyes were closed. It was as if he was petrified. She took

43

his belt off and threw it on the floor. In her head she knew exactly what she was doing. She knew exactly what she wanted.

She stood before Max and kissed him again. His dick was shiny and was as hard as a diamond. She walked backwards while pulling him by his dick. She fell back onto her couch. He was standing directly in front of her. She slipped him into her mouth again. He reached down and realized that she had no panties on. She was as wet and juicy as a peach preserved in syrup. He pulled back, got on his knees before her and licked her from perineum to clit. Her pussy had a fragrance like uncut honey. She grabbed his face and pulled him close.

He was just about to enter her. "Do you have a condom?"

She paused. "Yes, I'll go get it."

On her way to get the condom she started having second thoughts. She opened Maurice's boxer drawer. She took out a strip of magnums, tore one off the strip and headed back to the living room. She had almost lost faith until she saw Max sitting on the couch with his dick in his hand and his eyes filled with eager anticipation. It was as if his dick had wiped her mind clean of her marriage.

She handed him the condom. And for a moment he hesitated. Then she hoisted up her skirt and he saw all that heaven. He slipped the condom on and she climbed on top of him. As he entered her she kissed him passionately and bit into his bottom lip.

And for the next fifteen minutes he was in and out of her in every which position.

All those years of circling and flirting added up to a whole lot of tension and when the tension broke, they both exploded simultaneously. Amanda was soaking wet, so was Max. They were out of breath. Now they had to deal with the aftermath.

"Shit, shit, shit. What are we doing?" Max felt guilty.

Amanda was not sure if she was guilty free. Finally she did not feel shackled to the idea of Maurice anymore.

She fell back onto the couch and said, "I don't know."

She started playing with her clit. Max looked over at her. She was still soaking wet. Max felt his dick getting hard again. She closed her eyes and reached into her juicy pussy. Max heard it make that slippery sound. He was rock hard again. His mind started racing. What if Maurice is on his way home?

"You have another condom?"

"Yes." She got up in a hurry, Max followed her.

The condom was on in no time and she was crouched over on the bed. Max tore into her this time with a passion. And she begged him to push harder. She wanted him to fuck her as if he wanted to hurt her. She wanted to remember this day for a very long time. Max just didn't want to be outdone. So they crashed into each other with reckless abandon.

This time only Max came. He was exhausted. So he stood above her and watched her play with her clit until she brought herself to climax. And *Bang*, they are back in the restaurant.

Max bit into his bottom lip thinking about how hard they fucked the last time. She slid her hand further up his thigh. The waiter walked over and handed them a dinner menu.

"We are just having drinks," Max was very curt.

"Ok," he handed them the drink menu. "The Merlot here is…"

"We'll have two," Amanda shot at him smiling, still reaching under the table.

Max slid down in his seat. Amanda felt the tip of his dick. She closed her eyes and took a deep breath.

"I want to suck your dick right now," she said with a certain amount of daring in her tone. Max could not believe what she just said.

"Ah," he was lost for words.
The waiter placed the two glasses of Merlot on the table. They finished both glasses before he could turn around.

"Check!" Max called out.

Amanda slipped out from behind the table and walked toward the door, Max's eyes followed her. She had a perfect apple shaped ass, her waist narrow, her hips wide and her legs extremely long. All he could think about was being inside of her. It was as if their thoughts were on auto-pilot.

She walked a half a block ahead of him. She knew exactly where she was going. The security at Mo's a few blocks down gave her the regular hassle at the door. She squeezed her way through the crowd, then to the back to the bathroom. Max was a steady distance behind her. He squeezed through the crowd barely being able to pass, because the people were so packed together by the reggae music.

He got to the bathroom door. He tried it. It was open. He went in slowly. Amanda smiled. She handed him a pair of panties. He put it to his nose. They were soaked with her juices. She placed one leg atop the toilet seat and bent over slightly. And in two seconds flat Max was inside her and they were huffing and moaning and trying their best to keep quiet.

Max reached around and placed two fingers in her mouth while he worked miracles from behind. Amanda could feel his balls slamming up against her clit as they kissed. She sucked on his lips harder the closer she came to having an orgasm. For Amanda having sex in this public place was enough for her to have an orgasm, but Max was so hard she felt he would pass out. She looked back at him in disbelief as he slid in and out of her. There was a knocking at the door. Max paused.

She looked back at him with anger in her eyes and mouthed the words, "You better not stop."

He grabbed a fist full of her hair and continued. His balls were knocking steadily against her hardened clit. He could feel her clenching around his dick. He pounded harder. She looked back in slow motion as she came.

As soon as she did she was like, "Ok, stop."

Max did not know what to do. So he grabbed his dick and finished the job. Amanda slipped out. And three minutes later Max followed. He got a text twenty minutes later saying, *"Thank you."*

Chapter Seven

Max jumped out of the cab in front of Vodou,
Brenton was standing on the sidewalk talking to a
young redhead. The conversation seemed casual.
Brenton spotted Max. They greeted each other.

"Hey Max, this is my friend, ah," he waited for
the young lady to chime in, but she didn't.

"Hey how are you Max, Brenton was just telling
me about you."

"Oh really?"

"Nah I was just telling her that I was here to meet
you, told her that we went to school together."

"Oh, okay cool." Max shot a look towards
Brenton. Brenton got the message, *"Who is the
white girl?"*

"She's an old friend, met her this morning."
They all laughed. There was an uncomfortable
silence.

"So it was good to see you again Brenton, I hope
we can hang out again soon."

"What are you doing later?" Brenton looked her
dead in the eyes.

She smiled and slid her fingers through her hair.

Brenton smiled. Yep. That was it. She bit her lip and looked him up and down. Later he'd be fucking her, again. Well that depended on how tonight turned out.

"So, I'll see you later?"

She said, "Yeah," in a teasing kind of way.

Max's eyes followed her round ass to the corner. Brenton watched Max watch her.

"Max, ain't you engaged?" Brenton spat out.

"Yeah but that doesn't mean I'm blind."

"Shit you'll be blind soon," Brenton laughed at Max for a few seconds.

"You been inside?" Max asked.

"Nah, just got here like two minutes before you."

"Who is, that chick?"

"That girl? Nobody."

"You fuckin' her right?" Max had a little envy in his voice. Not envy, envy, he had the good kind of envy that said, damn I wish that was me.

"Fuckin' no, fucked, yes. I need to get up in that a few more times before I can categorize it as fuckin'."

"She got a sweet ass for a white girl."

"Tell me about it, I don't know if it's Brooklyn or if it's the water but these white bitches be giving these sistahs a run for their money." Max agreed silently.

He did not like the word bitch very much, but Brenton was his boy so he didn't want to make an issue of it.

50

"Let's go get a drink man," Brenton said itching for a drink.

"Bet, Sophie and Meghan will be coming by soon."

"Damn." Brenton didn't want to see Meghan for the obvious reasons.

They sat on a low cushioned bench with their backs facing the street. Vodou was the spot where the people who were almost aged out of the scene hung out. They were a little too old to be *'clubbing'* but not old enough to be in bed by ten.

They were a room full of well bellied men. Their stomachs pushed aggressively against their cheap button downs. The women were a demented hybrid of skanks and matrons, dressed like conservative strippers. Skin tight tube dresses just above the knees. Twenty inch heels and the most outrageous fingernails, yet they sat in very tight pussy clusters, playing coy. They only became fully animated when top forty songs were played, the songs doubled as the fountain of youth. If you knew all the lyrics to *Niggas in Paris,* that automatically knocked ten years off your dead end life.

The place itself was not that bad. It was just strange being on the corner of Nostrand and Halsey, in the middle of the hood. In Manhattan this place would be pretty swank, but since it was in the hood it was hard to even take their attempts at being upscale seriously. They ordered drinks. Max nursed his beer. Brenton was on his second rum and coke when Sophie and Meghan came in. They were in good spirits. Sophie seemed looser than her normal uptight self. Brenton and Meghan were in a serious standoff. They did exchange pleasantries, but beyond that, their guns were drawn. Sophie was cozying up to Max. Meghan's mind slipped back to the bathroom a few hours ago. She smiled at Sophie.

"So how are you doing Meghan, haven't seen you since our last party on the fourth of July."

Max tried to take the words back just as they left his mouth. He remembered that that may not be the best thing to talk about right now.

"Yeah, I've been busy, work is kicking my ass."

"Are you still at that publishing company?"

"Yeah, we're getting ready to do the Frankfurt book fair and it's so much..."

"Frankfurt? Nice." Max shot back not really paying attention.

Sophie was more touchy feely than she normally would have been. She was rubbing Max's thigh really slowly. She was thinking about Meghan's mouth against her clit. She shuddered. It was a flashback from earlier.

"Damn the AC is cold," she used as her cover.

"You want me to warm you up?" Max put his arm around Sophie.

Meghan looked across the small table at Brenton. He was on his fourth rum and coke and Meghan was looking super sexy in her work/party clothes.

Meghan worked in party clothes. He thought about the stairwell and in that same moment Meghan's mind went to the same place. They shared a resistant smile. Sophie whispered something to Max. Max rubbed her cheek with his nose.

"Anybody want anything? I'm going to get another rum and coke," Brenton asked.

He only got up because he wanted to give Max and Sophie a moment by themselves.

"Stella," Max uttered.

By now Sophie did not care she just said, "Red wine."

Meghan followed Brenton. "You owe me an apology Mister." She stuck him in the side playfully.

He turned and grabbed onto her finger. She tried to get loose. And that gentle tugging of her finger came to mean something entirely different to both of them. They were both aroused by the playful gesture. The unspoken sexual tension was obvious so Brenton let her finger go. She wanted him to continue. He knew it but he would not, just yet.

"What are you having?"

"Pinot."

"You like Pinot?" He said with a smile on his face.

She made a face at him. He stood by the edge of the bar trying to get the bartenders attention. Meghan pressed her groin area flush against his thigh.

"Why is she playing," Brenton thought to himself.

Max saw her pressed against Brenton, and thought to himself, *"Only Brenton could have pulled that off."*

Sophie saw her pressed against him and a huge wave of jealousy rode through her body.

Brenton took Meghan's face in his right hand and got as close to her as he could and said, "Why are you playing with me?"

She looked back at him, took his face in both her hands and said, "I am *NOT* playing."

The DJ started playing *Night Nurse* by Gregory Isaacs and Brenton pretended Meghan was not grinding against his thigh. His dick was a solid bar of steel in his pants. Meghan was in her own world, she was lost in the song. She had totally forgotten all about Brenton fucking her sister.

"You should come home with me," she whispered.

She wanted someone to make her curl the way she made Sophie curl. She wanted someone to make her cum the way she made Sophie cum. She knew Brenton was the man for the job.

Brenton turned to her; they were now face to face. He kissed her gently on her mouth; her lips were a little tangy. It was a mix of wine and something else; he could not quite put his finger on it. But he loved the taste. They kissed again. If he did not know better he would say her lips tasted like vagina, *"No way,"* he let the thought go.

The bartender finally came over; by that time they had given up or were too turned on to care. Meghan was half way out the door with Brenton close behind. The alcohol was rummaging through their bodies. Meghan had made her decision she was going to fuck Brenton tonight, whether he wanted her to or not.

She dragged him into a cab. It was only a few blocks to her apartment. Her blouse was half way off by the time he pushed her up against her door. She jangled the door knob with her key trying her best to get it in the hole; her breasts were already in his mouth. She cupped his head with one hand. She was grinding extremely hard against his dick. She wanted it inside her, wanted it in her mouth, in her hands, in her pussy, in her arm pits, in her lungs, in her everything. She wanted to fuck without promises or excuses. She knew she did not want him, she just wanted to fuck.

They stumbled into the living room. They were tearing the clothes off each other. Kissing. One arm out of her blouse. His pants were stuck; he could not get them over his shoes. He was trying to get his shoe off, it seemed impossible. She had his dick in her hand. His hand was up her skirt. She was super wet. They blindly made their way toward her bedroom, bumping into small pieces of furniture.

The light from the guest room came on. They

froze in place. Like a deer at a sex club. Her right
hand on his dick, his left hand up her skirt, their lips
locked, his pants around his ankles, her blouse half
way off, her left hand opening the door. Her sister
pushed the door open and the light hit them both.
She was drunk.

"What are you two doing?" she said as she
stumbled out the room half naked. "I have to go to
the bathroom, hey Meg, hey you. Do I know you?"
She had a puzzled look on her face.

She had a body like nothing Brenton had ever
seen. Her breasts were perfect and full of life and,
her ass was a wonder of the world; it seemed to
defy all logic. His dick got even harder.

She stopped halfway to the bathroom. "Wait, I
know you, how do I know you?" she slurred with a
confused look on her face.

They un-froze, Meghan pushed her room door
open. They fell into the room and onto her bed.
Brenton is almost always a hundred percent safe,
but tonight he was being a little careless. Meghan
was also being careless, she could hear her pussy
throbbing in her ears and all she wanted was to sit
on his dick.

She shoved him further onto the bed. Brenton
was focused on getting his pant leg over his shoe.
Meghan gave him an awkward angled blow job.
He finally got his pant over his shoe. She ended
her sucking routine with a popping, sucking sound.
In her mind she was like a professional gymnast

sticking a landing. She smiled.

He was blurry eyed, and half smiling. He sat up on the bed; she climbed onto his dick and slowly settled in, plunging all the way down. His hands found the flesh of her ass and she rode him slowly, her skirt rumpled around her waist. Brenton closed his eyes and slipped in and out of consciousness as he slipped in and out of her tight, wet pussy.

Something about her work clothes was an aphrodisiac. She found the zip of her skirt, unzipped it and pulled it over her head. She pressed her clit against his stomach muscle and grabbed the back of his head as he spread her wider and wider with each stroke. He slipped a finger into her ass as she gyrated. She gyrated harder. Her clit was humming. The sound of his dick squishing into and out of her was a carnal orchestra.

He opened his eye and standing in the door eating a sandwich, wobbling and watching him fuck the living daylights out of Meghan was Meghan's sister. Meghan was too focused on her orgasm to even notice, or even care.

Meghan knew exactly how to get hers and she had no qualms about it. She had shifted into third gear; her ass was moving like a rabbit. Her body was filled with beautiful motion, she pressed her lips against Brenton's and slid her tongue into his mouth and kissed him with all she had as a warm sensation walked up her spine. And *Bang*.

She exploded. Brenton's lap was covered with

her juices. He had never had a woman squirt in his lap before. It was a little strange, he was a little skeeved out, but he needed to get his. He flipped her onto her stomach and hoisted her pelvis with a pillow and dug in. Meghan moaned and positioned her ass so she could receive the best of his stroke.

He stroked her from behind with a magnificent vengeance, every stroke was an opus, and her moans confirmed that she wanted him deeper and harder. And just when he was about to come she slipped out from under him and took the entire load into her mouth.

She was exhausted. He was exhausted. She licked her lips and gently sucked on the tip of his dick until she fell asleep. He sat up and watched her for a few moments, is body was giddy with spasms.

Chapter Eight

It was Saturday, late summer. The blue dust of August was smeared on the face of everything visible. The evening was sluggish. Maurice sat quietly at the bar. The humidity outside was pretty oppressive by any standard. He was having his regular, a mango-mango. When he was not out partying, he liked drinking girlie drinks.

He was holed up in the Brooklyn Moon waiting for his boys, Max and Brenton. He was closer friends with Max because Max had mentored him when he was at Syracuse. He met Brenton through Max and over the years they had all become less like friends and more like brothers.

Maurice was mulling over a look he saw on Amanda's face before he left the house that morning. He felt something was awry. She was up to something, what it was he did not know but it bothered him.

There was an uproar by the door. Maurice spun around; it was Max and Daren. Daren was Amanda's younger brother. Let's just say Maurice did not like Daren very much. Why? Daren was an attention whore. He had been an attention whore since he was a kid, and as an adult it was an addiction he could not break.

Maurice braced himself as he uttered, "This mothafucka," under his breath.

Daren was causing a ruckus by the door. "These people in here are not here to see you boo boo." He gestured broadly as he pranced past Max.

Max shook his head. "It's not like they're here to see you!"

"Why did I say that?" Max thought to himself.

He had just poured a whole tank of gasoline on an inferno waiting to rage, that was literally begging for more fuel so it could just swallow everything in sight.

"Uh uhhhhhhh, you did not, did you... did you say what I just thought you said...?" Daren was getting ready to tear into Max.

Maurice hurried from the bar to make peace. "Yo, yo, yo fellas come on, calm down man, let's go get these drinks."

The bartender saw Max. He hurried to the fridge. Before they could be seated Max had an ice cold Stella waiting for him.

The Brooklyn Moon was Max's favorite place to hang; it was all their favorite place to eat and favorite place to meet up with friends. Max loved *The Moon* mainly because it was like going home. The owner knew him personally, he knew the entire staff, and they were like family to him. Most of all he loved The Moon because he could always talk to Mike, the owner about his problems.

Max's phone made a sound. He looked at it. Maurice and Daren were having verbal skirmish.

"Why can't you just chill man?" Maurice was trying to reach Daren without sounding preachy.

"Why I gotta chill for?" Daren fired back with bite in his tone.

"I'm just saying sometimes you don't have to make a scene." Maurice was trying to back away, he saw where this was heading and he was heading for the tonal exit.

"What, you trying to say I am always loud, is that it?" Daren said being obviously loud.

"Dude, dude listen no one is saying you are loud, I'm just saying if you just chill sometimes maybe you would have a better time." Maurice was impressed with himself; he had a smile budding in the corner of his mouth.

Daren gave him the side eye. "Well everybody 'chills' differently, I have to be who I am."

"You know what, you are right," Maurice said quietly. "What are you drinking?"

Max was tempted by the text. It was from Amanda. It simply said, *"Come over."* His dick jumped in his pants. He looked at Maurice navigating Daren's psyche. He hated himself for wanting to go and fuck his best friend's wife. He hated himself for cheating on Sophie, but Amanda had that edge.

He texted back, *"Why?"*

Daren looked over the drink menu. "These drinks are cheeeep," Daren dragged out his last word.

Max and Maurice looked at each other. Maurice gave Max that look that said, *"Don't even,"* but Max could not help himself.

It was just the way he was and before he knew it he said, "Says the broke guy."

And without losing a beat went right back to his phone, a new message had just landed. Maurice tried his best to hold back laughter, Mike turned away and started laughing, Daren was about to explode.

Maurice grabbed his hand. "Dude, you know he's playing right? He's just trying to get under your skin, don't fall for it man, don't fall for it."

Daren took a deep breath and did his *'keep it together sign'* with his fingers.

"Like I was saying," he went on, "can I have two shots of Grey Goose and a vodka soda since Mr. Big Shot here is paying."

Max did not even hear that he was paying. He had serious decisions to make.

The text that landed said, *"Because my pussy is wet and waiting."*

Max looked over at Maurice mulling over his drink. "Where is Brenton?" Max asked.

"He said he'd be here a little late," Maurice replied, his brows knitted.

"Is he ever early?" Daren fired out.

"He is kinda always late," Max acknowledged.

He was trying to decide what to do. And just when he was about to send Amanda a text saying he was hanging with Maurice at the Brooklyn Moon his phone rang. It was Amanda. He stepped away from the bar and walked toward the door speaking quietly into the phone.

Over the phone Amanda was making her case. "You don't even have to stay for ten minutes. I just want you to come over here and fuck me real swift and real hard, you don't even have to say hello, I'll leave the door open. You just come in. I'll be bent over on the couch. Just come in, fuck me and leave." She said it just the way she imagined one of the heroines in the romantic novels she loved so much would say it.

The texture of her voice licked all sense of reasoning off of Max's dick. "I'll be there in five."

Before she could press the end call button on her phone Max was on Myrtle Ave. His car screeched to a stop a few doors down from the Five Spot. He did not want to park in front of Maurice's townhouse on Washington.

Max dipped around the corner like a thief and true to her word the door was open. The knob turn in his hand was a divine feeling that released waves of sexual energy inside Max's body. He walked down the hall and just as she promised Amanda was kneeling on the edge of the couch looking away from the door.

Brenton walked into the Brooklyn Moon. "Yow, what's up?" He gave both Daren and Maurice the obligatory greetings.

"Where's Max? That dude is always late man."

"I think he went outside, phone call, I don't know, he's out there." Maurice was still trying to figure out that look on Amanda's face.

A chill came over his body. *"She wants a divorce,"* he thought to himself. *"That was it. No."* He was not sure.

Max walked gingerly toward Amanda's beautiful fleshy ass. He could see that the lips of her vagina were glistening. He licked his lips, caught the tip of his tongue with his index and middle fingers a few times and gently slid them through Amanda's pussy. She purred. She moaned. She rotated her hips and dropped the middle of her back while hoisting her ass higher to make her pussy more available to him.

Without a word she reached back and handed him a condom; Magnum. He slipped the condom on and fucked her exactly how she wanted to be fucked; mercilessly. All he could think about while he was fucking her was his boy, Maurice. Max was dying inside, but the slapping sounds quickly gave him amnesia. He was ashamed to be doing this but Amanda's pussy and her propositions were irresistible.

With every stroke his dick grew harder. With

every stroke her pussy grasped him tighter.
Amanda knew exactly what she was doing. Max
was in a kind of silent heaven. A heaven he
promised would call him Jesus before this was
over. A heaven so tight it almost pulled the
condom off his dick.

He made sure the condom was in place then lifted
one leg on the edge of the couch and continued.
His balls slamming gently against her clit was like
Judas knocking at the gates of heaven. Amanda
grunted as he went deeper and deeper. She was
trying her best not to make a sound.

He grabbed a fist full of her hair and went harder.
He could hear the word building in her throat. She
was in a semi-squeal. Max was having an out of
body experience. He was almost there. It was as if
the world around him was frozen and he was just
going in and out, in and out, in and out, in and out,
to the side, to the side, to the side, to the side. His
nut was building; he could feel that sweet tickle
below his balls. And *Bang*. Amanda felt the
vibration that came off Max's dick as he ejaculated
inside of her, sending shock waves flying through
her.

She fell into a spell of spasms and as the waves
slowly subsided. "Oh, oh, oh, oh, oh Jesus."

She was bathed in a holy feeling. She mumbled
to herself in a strange tongue. Max had just filled
her with the Holy Ghost it seemed. This was the
best not-orgasm she had ever had in her life. And

just like that he zipped his pants, fixed his shirt, dabbed the sweat from his face and vanished out the door like a phantom.

Chapter Nine

Max was back at the Brooklyn Moon in less than five minutes.

The evening was still young and there was a ton to catch up on and there were millions of drinks to be consumed, and God was somewhere watching.

Max could still smell Amanda's pussy on his fingertips. The memories of her heart shaped ass propped up on that couch stayed with him; he played with his nose all night. He did not want to get Amanda's pussy out of his head.

"So what's the plan for the night guys?" Mike asked wiping down the bar.

"I don't know, Mo's later on," Maurice answered.

"Definitely Mo's." Brenton seemed thrilled.

"Mo's? Really? Mo's?" Daren did not like the sound of it.

They all looked at Daren.

"What? Mo's is so ghetto," Daren said emphatically.

"Kinda like you," Max uttered under his breath. Daren pretended he did not hear him.

"Two more shots of Grey Goose please Mike. If

I'm going to Mo's I'm gonna have to be drunk before I get there." Daren sat like a Cheshire cat with a pot full of snobbery in his lap.

Brenton looked at Daren. "How did you get here tonight?" he asked quizzically.

"I walked," Daren replied.

"No, I mean, how? Like how did you get to be here? This is kind of our boy's night out. Normally it's just the three of us, you know, chillin." Brenton was being a little harsh.

"Whatever, Amanda told me I could come hang with ya'll. We were in the house all day; guess she needed some space or whatever. I'm not even here to hang out with you; I'm here to hang with my brother-in-law," Daren said dryly.

Maurice gave him the side eye. He knew what had happened. Daren had worn out Amanda's ear all day so she passed him off to them. Now no matter how much they wanted to just chill they knew tonight was not going to be the same.

Brenton smiled to himself, as he watched Daren throw back the second of two shots. Brenton had a plan.

"Yo Mike, double shots of Patron for everybody." Brenton slipped Mike a $100 without anyone seeing.

Mike gave them a round. The guys threw the first round back. Their glasses were replenished. They threw back the second round. Mike immediately refilled Daren's glass without Daren noticing.

Daren looked at the filled glass confused, he was not sure if he had had one or two shots.

"Dude, drink up man, you said you wanted to hang with the boys right?" Maurice hit him lightly with his elbow.

Max caught onto what was happening. He smiled to himself; the shots were beginning to work. Daren emptied his glass.

Mike was in a good mood it seemed. "You know what fellas, one more round, this one is on me."

"Let's go," Brenton said slapping his palm against the bar.

"Let's do it," Max uttered rubbing his hands together.

"I thought you were ready to roll Daren, what's up?" Maurice teased.

"I, I, I am ready! Listen I am gonna drink every last one of you girls under the table." His words were beginning to slur a bit.

Mike made a special concoction, and by the look on his face this one was the killer. He poured. They drank. He poured again. They drank again. There was not a hint of alcohol in the concoction. The boys threw them back with ease. They ended up doing about three more shots than they had originally planned. Mike was all smiles.

They got up to head over to Mo's; turned out standing was not a good idea. They were standing on strange legs. Daren was flat drunk. He could barely walk. The plan was to park him in a chair inside of Mo's while they partied.

Chapter Ten

They crawled out into the Brooklyn night. The humidity was a perfect, thick sheet of summer pressed down from the darkened sky. The night air was filled with desires and wants. Everyone they passed seemed to be on the prowl. They ran into a group of old friends and stood around for a few minutes talking about nothing. They also decided that Mo's was a good idea. Mo's was packed beyond any kind of human recognition. Sardines would be an understatement. Brenton squeezed his way through the crowd. He ended up face to face with the redhead.

"Are you stalking me?" Brenton asked smiling as he rubbed up against her.

"Not yet," she said looking him up and down as a pair of soft hands slinked around her waist from behind her.

The redhead pulled Brenton closer. *"Life is good, but it can't be this good,"* Brenton thought to himself. Before he knew it he was being caressed by two sets of hands.

"Who is your friend?" Brenton asked.

"This is my friend Maria, she's visiting from Miami," the redhead yelled.

"It's easier if you whisper," Brenton whispered into her ear.

"What?"

"I can hear you better if you whisper."

Maria took Brenton's hand into her palm. Her palms were a little damp.

Brenton's mind went straight to her crotch. *"Her pussy must be so juicy,"* he thought to himself.

They were all so full of alcohol, and the music was just pounding against their bodies that the only thing they could think of was fucking. But it was illegal to fuck on the dance floor so they tried their best to do everything except.

Maria pulled Brenton behind her. The redhead turned around and faced Maria. They started making out. Brenton felt her ass pressing against his raging erection. Maria took his hand and placed it on her thigh then slipped it between herself and the redhead. She pressed his fingers into her lap while she gyrated. He felt the plush juicy mound of flesh and almost lost his mind. The redhead pulled him into their kiss. Max was amazed.

Maurice was dancing with a young lady with a nice respectful distance between. Daren was fast asleep out front on one of the couches snoring up a storm. The song ended. Maria and the redhead did not notice. They kept grinding, they kept kissing. Brenton was the envy of the entire room. A few guys even gave him approving looks. He shot them a wink.

His index finger and middle finger were fully married to the insides of Maria's juicy pussy, while his left hand had a full pound of the redhead's ass crying out for dear mercy.

DJ Hard Hittin Harry. DJ Hard Hittin Harry droned out the speakers. Then came Prince's, *I Wanna Be Your Lover*. Half way into the first line the redhead had had enough.

"Let's go to my place," she said eagerly.

They hurried out through the side door. Brenton didn't even say goodbye. His boys understood. This was kind of a long standing tradition. They would all go out. They would all get drunk. They would go home to their women and Brenton would go home with some chick he met that night.

They stumbled into 99 Lafayette, at no point did they ever let go of each other. They choreographed a beautiful walking kiss. The elevator was one of those old elevators that could barely fit five people. In the middle of kissing Maria slipped down onto her knees, between Brenton and the redhead, Brenton and the redhead were so focused on each other it was as if Maria was not even there.

"Mmmm, no panties," Maria licked her lips as she claimed a mouth full of the redhead's clit. She rubbed her hand along the front of Brenton's pants. "Mmmm, you are packing there mister," she mumbled with her mouth full.

Before she could unzip his pants the elevator bell rang. Ding. She shot up. Brenton was kissing the redhead's neck. Maria pulled them slowly by their hands toward the apartment door. She could barely keep her balance in the narrow hallway. The redhead handed Maria her keys. Maria joined in the kiss for a few seconds before she opened the door. That kiss served as a *don't leave me out of this* to both Brenton and the redhead. Brenton was truly looking forward to this re-acquaintance.

They entered the dimly lit apartment. Brenton paused as Maria took the redhead into her arms. He let them kiss for a while, for now he just wanted to watch. Their kiss was getting more and more intense. The music from the club was still in Brenton's body. Something in the back of his mind kept telling him he was missing an amazing party.

Maria shoved the redhead onto the bed. She fell back giggling. Her tube dress was the perfect length just below her ass, so that as she fell the entire mouth of her vagina was exposed. She wiggled a bit as she eased the dress over her ass and spread her legs slowly. Maria crawled toward her like a panther stalking her prey. The redhead was breathing slowly.

Maria's dress rode up over her ass and exposed what looked like a perfectly shaped diamond cleft of vagina being held together by the thin fabric of her underwear. Brenton unzipped his pants and held his dick in his hand. The sound of his zipper

74

got the attention of Maria and the redhead. Maria looked back and saw him, his dick bursting with tension.

She cupped the redhead's ass with both hands and pulled her closer then she used her right hand to shift her panties to the side. She was soaking wet. If it was possible Brenton got even harder. Brenton took his thumb and pressed it downward in Maria's pussy and moved it around gently across her g-spot. He could tell he was hitting the spot by the sounds Maria made; by the way she moved her body when he hit a certain place. He bit into her ass cheek. He pulled his thumb out and wiped the juices across the redhead's lips.

Maria flashed her hair from side to side as she planted her head into the redheads pussy and pressed her tongue slowly into the sweet tangy rift and valleys and flicked her clit a few times before she looked up and asked, "You like that?"

The redhead gyrated upward as Maria planted her head in her crotch once again.

Brenton took his shirt off, then his pants. He had no underwear on. Had something to do with touring and not wanting to worry about having clean underwear. He joined Maria as she feasted on the redhead's clit. They took turns. Then they got their strategy together. Maria dove deep with her tongue while Brenton focused on the clit.

As the intensity built in her loins the redhead reached out and pulled Brenton onto her face. She took his balls into her mouth, while she jerked his dick. Maria saw this and joined in. While Brenton straddled the redhead's face Maria sucked the meaning out of his dick, he reached over her back and fingered her quietly from behind. Brenton got a little uncomfortable when the redhead flicked her tongue through his ass. The sensation was good but it was not his cup of tea.

In his mind Brenton was like, *"What the fuck. Why is this even an issue? I am here with two chicks and I'm thinking- her putting her tongue in my ass is gay?"*

Before Brenton could have another thought Maria started kissing him. He pulled her closer as she removed her tube dress.

All Maria kept thinking was she wanted his dick inside of her. She slowly coaxed him off of the redhead's face and laid him down on his back and straddled him. They were still kissing. The redhead felt left out. Maria reached back and took his dick into her hand and was about to plunge it deep inside of herself when she felt another hand. It was the redhead.

"I hope she is not thinking what I think she is thinking," Maria thought to herself. Turned out the redhead wasn't. She took Brenton's dick into her mouth and gave it a few once overs to make sure it was nice and ready. Maria looked back and smiled a naughty smile as the redhead slipped a condom into her mouth and with no hands slowly unfurled it

onto Brenton's dick. Maria's heart pounded with expectation as the redhead gently placed it inside of Maria's warm, wet, dripping pussy. As Maria slid down the redhead took Brenton's balls into her mouth. Brenton was in heaven.

Maria thought about her ex-boyfriend and how he was never open to something like this. The redhead was in total bliss; she and Maria had been lovers for many years, they had always spoken about having a threesome but never knew how to put it to their respective boyfriends. So here they were both fulfilling a deep desire while sharing a special moment with each other.

The redhead hugged Maria from behind and kissed the nape of her neck as Maria rode Brenton at a slow and steady pace.

Chapter Eleven

The night slugged on, Brenton was still passed out next to the bodies of the two beautiful women. He somehow managed to open his eyes, the drinks Mike had made were stronger than he had expected.

He looked at the two women and smiled, *"Fuck, what's her name again?"* Why couldn't he remember her name? His brain went back to the moment he saw the redhead and this other chick at Mo's.

"Who is your friend?" Brenton had asked as the redhead pulled him closer.

"This is my friend...," the sound of the music made mush out of her words.

Brenton's head was still a little knotted with alcohol. He laid back and thought to himself, *"Fuck it."*

His phone rang in his pants on the floor. He reached over Maria into the pocket of his pants. It was Max texting.

"Where you at?" the text said.

Brenton was too spent to waste time texting, so he turned off his phone.

It was about 2:30 am, and in the front section of Mo's there was a raucous. Daren woke up and realized that he had been stranded. He was livid, so he started asking random people questions.

"Hey, Hey, Hey ma man nobody out here knows who your friends are, I'ma need you to calm down in here a'ight." The security guy was about six eight and menacing.

Daren knew his drama would not work in a situation like this. Everyone at the bar was looking at him.

He had slept off most of the alcohol but he was still a little drunk. "I'm just sayin' I came here with three guys and I want to know where they are."

"Listen here man, you should be lucky I ain't thrown your ass out a long time ago with all that snoring you was doing up in here." The security guy stepped forward.

"Me, snore-I do not snore ok." Daren gave him a scornful look.

"Why don't you go look in the back, see if your friends are back there?"

Daren hissed his teeth and tramped off. "That's what I was about to do, I don't need you to tell me that."

The truth is Daren was totally discombobulated when he woke up and went directly to 'abandoned child' mode.

When he got to the back Max was pressed up against a young lady and so was Maurice. And next to them was a very plump little miss, looking extremely lonely. She was not exactly fat but not exactly in shape either. Almost everyone in the back room at this time of night was grinding on someone else. This was where most folks made their closing arguments.

DJ Hard Hittin Harry was playing lover's rock. Harry owned the audience with every new song he played: *DJ Hard Hittin Harry, Harry, Harry* broke through the speakers. Then just like that he dropped the beat. It was as if Harry scooped a thick dose of nostalgia out of his sonic archives and poured it into the room. *No, No No...you don't love me and I know now...* The crowded room sang along.

Everyone was fully animated; they could taste the song on their tongues. They seemed to grind harder and with even more intent. Daren moved in on the lonely young lady and by the second line of the song he was engaged in a full frontal grind session.

The strangest thing about Daren was that alcohol freed him from all inhibitions and this young lady was very thankful. Three songs deep and they were fully engaged in a deep tongue kiss. Max and Maurice were shocked.

They kept looking at each other and looking at Daren as if to say, *"I thought he was gay."*

An hour later the party was winding down. Max and Maurice were standing close to the side exit.

They had abandoned their dance partners. They had women waiting at home.

"We should leave him," Max said in a semi-whisper.

"Nah, I can't. He is my insurance policy," Maurice replied.

"Your, what?"

"Insurance, you see the time right?"

"Yeah."

"It's 3:30am. If he was not here I would have been home a long time ago."

"Oh, Oh I get it…"

Daren and his plump friend were the only ones left grinding on the dance floor.

Chapter Twelve

"So you are saying that Max is tired of me?" Sophie said with a look of disgust on her face.

"No I am not saying he is tired of you, he has just gotten used to you." Her therapist spoke with a firm calm voice.

This was Sophie's first trip to a therapist, a sex therapist at that. Meghan had convinced her so she decided she was going to give this therapy thing a test run before she got Max involved.

"So what do I do, it's not like I can change that, because I am always going be me."

"That's your answer, sometimes don't be you." The therapist opened a hole in Sophie's head.

"Don't be me, what, what is that supposed to mean?"

Sophie understood but she didn't know how to not be Sophie; the well-coiffed almost militarized personality, with every strand of hair in place, with her schedules and deadlines and meeting times always in the front of her mind. She didn't know how to relax.

"Have you ever role played Sophie?"

"Yes, I studied theatre at Clark," she said with an almost august sense of self.

"How about in the bedroom, have you ever role played in the bed."

"Of course not," she said with disgust. "The theatre is …." She was searching for the word to describe the elevated feelings she had for the theatre.

"Sophie, use that skill and love for the theatre to save your relationship."

Sophie was a little confused by the therapist's statements but she was desperate.

"So what do you suggest I do?" she said quietly.

"Role play; inject a little excitement in your relationship. Be different people for him; make it your little game." Ms. Claremont had a sly smile jammed in the corner of her mouth as she said this.

She was well put together in her skirt suit. To the untrained eye she was just another psychologist who was into books and ideas on how human beings think about things, but to the trained eye, beneath all that well manicured posterior was a woman who knew her way around a bedroom. She was a woman who was open in ways most women could not even begin to conceive.

Sophie was mulling over what Ms. Claremont said. *Make it your little game.* And *Bang*.

Sophie is dressed like a stripper with one leg cocked atop the arm of the couch as Max walks through the door. It is almost four in the morning.

Max is still a little drunk. *"This can't be real,"* he is thinking. Sophie walks toward him seductively in her crotch-less, full body, fishnet get up.

"Sophie?" Max inquired.

"Who's Sophie?" she replied, she had become someone else.

She said it so convincingly that she almost believed it. Max was turned on by the proposition. She grabbed him by the tongue of his belt and pulled him toward the couch. She barely spoke and when she did she always referred to him as Big Boy. Sophie had never been into sucking dick. But tonight Sophie was not home. She was a stripper she had hired to treat her fiancé to a good time.

She slowly used her teeth to unzip his pants. She could see the bulge getting bigger and bigger. She used her mouth to undo the button at the waist. Max was in awe.

"Where did you learn this?"

"Shhhhh." Her head stayed in his lap as her right index finger pressed against his lips.

With that Max sat back, who was he to complain, this was not the time to ask questions. After that moment Max experienced what may have been the best blow job he had ever had. It was not so much that she sucked his dick; it was more like she made love to it.

He could not begin to think of words of appreciation, all he could think of was, *"How do I return the favor?"* Sophie didn't want the favor returned. For now Max would have to owe her.

She walked toward the bedroom switching her ass, stopped in the doorway of the bedroom and called him slowly.

"You ready for round two big boy?"

The light gleaming off her ass, the seduction in her voice, the crotch-less bodysuit, this strange act, the way she switched-- all of it made Max want to fuck. Not fuck like boring everyday fuck. He wanted to fuck like new coochie fuck. Fuck like a porn star. And fuck he did.

Chapter Thirteen

Sophie looked at herself in the mirror. She was not too happy with what she saw. She was getting up there in age and the wrinkles around her mouth and talons by her eyes were becoming pronounced. Well the truth is it was not really the wrinkles but she would blame them anyway.

She touched her stomach softly, then stood sideways and puffed out her stomach. She wondered what a small version of herself would look like. She wondered if she would get fat like so many women she knew. She scrunched up her nose. She shook her head as if disagreeing with herself. There was no way she would get fat. There was a banging on the door. Sophie jumped.

"Come on honey I have to use the bathroom," Max was outside dying to pee.

"One second," she said quickly as she disrobed before clicking the bathroom door open.

Max rushed in. She positioned herself in front of the sink. She wanted something different this morning. The sound of his urine pouring into the toilet turned her on for some strange reason. Ever since that encounter with Meghan it was as if she was constantly horny. Meghan had somehow eased her out of her old mechanical self and all she could think about since then was how much she had been missing sexually. Before that night with Meghan, all she had known were missionary and the occasional doggy style, in bed of course. Since then and with the help of the therapist, her head was brimming with new and exciting ways to fuck her man.

She moaned a soft sweet moan, just to get his attention. She turned the water on and filled her palms and bent over to wash her face, just in time for Max to see the full apple of her ass.
Immediately he thought of Amanda on that couch. Sophie thought of Meghan for a split second. She imagined Meghan behind her nibbling on her clit. She pulled another palm full of water over her face. And *Bang.* It hit her.

The tip of Max's dick gently slid into her. She pressed back against him. She looked up from the sink and saw a slight smile in Max's eyes as he eased in and out of her gently.

"Fuck me Max," she said softly.

Max saw the intensity in her eye. He was a bit shocked. This was so unlike Sophie. Max in that moment just knew he had to be dreaming, *"Sophie doesn't speak like this,"* he thought to himself.

Was she channeling Amanda? Or was he channeling Amanda through Sophie?

"What?" he asked playfully.

"I want you to fuck me Max, fuck me like a whore."

This was what Max had wanted Sophie to be like, all these years, but he did not know how to tell her. How does someone say to their woman that he wants her to be more like a whore in bed? Max was beside himself. His dick was by far the hardest it had ever been his entire life.

He grabbed a fist full of her hair and looked her deep in the eyes through the mirror and said, "Ok."

And for the next forty five minutes he had her in every humanly possible position inside that bathroom. It was as if her words had rendered his dick twenty years younger. Sophie for the first time had an orgasm from penetration. She noticed that the dirtier she spoke the more intense his passion. She realized that she had finally found the key to Max's heart. All those years of etiquette at finishing school and they never once mentioned that she needed to talk dirty to her man to keep him excited. They ended on the side of the tub with Sophie in a trembling spasm and Max totally exhausted. It seemed like this was a new beginning for Sophie and Max.

Max slid off of Sophie and laid on the bathroom floor looking at the ceiling with a smile on his face. Had Sophie just fucked him the way he thought she did? Yes she did. His head was tumbling in every which way. *"Who is this strange woman ?"* he kept thinking to himself.

Chapter Fourteen

Maurice stumbled through the front door reeking of alcohol; right behind him was Daren and his 'friend' Sheila. Maurice meandered through the passage into the living room. It seemed as if he was getting drunker and drunker by the minute. Those shots from Mike had slowly crept up on him; it was as if the shots had been waiting for him to get home to start working.

"Dude, what are you doing with this girl man?" Maurice said barely audible, his eyes half shut.

Daren looked at him with disgust. "What do you mean?"

Maurice looked at the young lady. She was semi-drunk. Her eyes filled with wanting. She held onto Daren as if he was her long lost lover.

"So you not gonna tell her?"

Daren widened his eyes. "Tell her what?" he shot back. "We are just gonna stay down here and talk!" A little bit of his sass came out.

Maurice shot him a cold stare. "Whatever dude," and walked off.

Daren and Sheila sat on the couch where Max and Amanda had their episode. In truth Daren had no intention of having sex with Sheila; he just wanted to make out with her. Daren had this strange thing about him, whenever he drank it seemed he became straight or something like that. It was chemical; he had never been able to explain it but sometimes he thought that deep down he might be bi.

Maurice sat at the bottom of the stairs for about an hour before he dragged himself to his bed. He fell out cold as soon as he hit the sheets.

Sheila was not as drunk as she let on. She was running the game most women ran, she had planned to fuck someone tonight but she needed a cover. In the morning she could definitely say she was drunk.

After making out for an hour, she had to make her move. The sun was going to rise soon. She rubbed her hand slowly over Daren's dick while they kissed. Daren was turned on but he did not want to take it any further than just kissing. She used her other hand to undo her top. Her breasts were enormous. She pressed Daren's face into her cleavage. Daren loved breasts. He dove in and inhaled. He wanted to stop but she stuck one nipple into his mouth and patted his head while he sucked.

She kept rubbing the front of his pants. Then slowly she unzipped it. They started building a kind of rhythm between them. His dick was in her hand. Her nipple was in his mouth. He had her ass awkwardly in his grip. Her other hand was stuffed into her pussy digging and scooping at a flawless tempo. And *Bang.*

They both lost all sense of who they were, where they were and what they were doing. In one svelte motion they ended up in a sixty-nine position with Sheila on top with Daren's dick in her mouth. She sucked it with a vengeance. She had not seen or touched a real dick in ages. Daren looked up and saw the plump mound of flesh sticky with cream; he was a little skived out. But the Alcohol was speaking so he was like, *"fuck it"* and decided to go for it.

With his eyes closed and his heavy tongue barely out his mouth he slowly pressed his face upward but before he could get a taste he lost his nerve and chickened out. She pressed her entire undercarriage down onto his face. He shifted to the side. Her vagina slammed into his ear. Was her vagina loud? Yes it was - it was turned up to full volume.

He eased her off his head and slowly stuffed two fingers into her, then three, then four, then, "Oooooh shit!" Daren had never had his dick sucked like this.

She sucked his dick with such reckless abandon that it inspired him. He curved his fingers in on her g-spot and went to work. They did not realize it but they were making so much noise that they woke Amanda.

Amanda was on her way downstairs. Daren and

Sheila were so engaged that they did not hear a thing. All they knew was each other. She licked and sucked and he entered and exited her, with a kind of primal randomness that was beautiful. And just as Daren hit Sheila's sweet spot and she felt the power of a damning orgasm raging through her body she arched her back like a cat and squeezed her cheeks as tight as she could and took Daren's entire dick into her mouth and slowly eased back and right there in that moment, Amanda stepped into the living room. And *Bang*. Daren shot off into Sheila's mouth. Sheila gagged and raised her head and looked Amanda dead in the eyes with her mouth full of warm cum.

Amanda hissed at her. "What the fuck?" Rolled her eyes and tramped off.

Sheila did not know what to do or say. Daren was in a daze, he did not fully realize what had happened. He knew someone had walked in on them but he was too exhausted to think about it so he just passed out from exhaustion and started snoring.

Chapter Fifteen

Brenton woke up and scanned the room. It was in total disarray. Where was he, what had happened the night before. It all started flooding back to him. He noticed the two young women. His head was pounding. Fuck, what time was it? He reached over Maria to get his phone on the floor. She half woke up and moaned a bit. It was 8:30am. He had not missed his meeting with KEV.

Maria rubbed his chest and snuggled up to him. He ran his fingers through her hair. She kissed his chest lightly. He gave out a little sound egging her on. She continued going lower and lower and lower. He looked over at the redhead. She was still asleep. He ran his fingers through her hair. She took a deep breath and rolled over toward Brenton. She opened her eyes, looked up at Brenton and smiled.

"Last night was fun," she muttered just as she noticed the sheets moving up and down, up and down, up and down.

"It was-good-old- A-me-ri-can fun." Maria was definitely disrupting his concentration.

"What is she doing?" the redhead said playfully.

"I have no idea, I think you should check on her," Brenton said with a half-smile.

"I think I just might do that mister," as she slid down below the sheets.

Brenton pulled the sheets over his head and watched as Maria and the redhead took turns with his dick.

"You done well for yourself, Brenton Allen," he thought. The redhead decided it was time to move things forward; she reached into a drawer from her side table and pulled out a condom. And *Bang.*

Chapter Sixteen

Breakfast at Amanda's and Maurice's was extremely awkward. One reason being Amanda had seen something she could not believe. Maurice did not know how to bring up what happened with Daren and Sheila at the club. So they sat at the table chewing quietly.

"So how was last night?" Amanda asked Maurice while looking at Daren.

Daren had the nastiest look possible on his face. He came to the realization that Amanda was the one who had walked in on him and Sheila; he hated the way Amanda was going about torturing him.

"Was a good night, we went to the Moon then to Mo's."

"Mo's, why Mo's?" she said almost scornfully.

"I was saying the same thing," Daren finally spoke.

"You were saying a lot of things Daren," Maurice said messing around.

Daren wanted no part of it. He rolled his eyes and focused on his eggs.

"What happened to that girl, ah what's her name? Damn, I think I had too much to drink last night."

Amanda looked at Maurice bewildered. "Tell me something new."

Maurice knew exactly what she meant. "I really need to quit."

"You say that every time you go drinking."

Amanda got up from the table to go get the ketchup.

"Dude what happened to that girl?" Maurice asked Daren this time looking into his eyes to see if Daren would lie.

"We really gon' go there?"

"I'm just saying."

"Well she went home," Daren said not wanting to venture any further.

"Did you?" Maurice made the signal for fucking with his finger and hand. The whole time he was laughing.

"What the fuck do you mean?" Daren was livid, he was beside himself; he had that how dare you look on his face.

"I'm just playing," Maurice said still laughing.

Amanda sat back down.

"What are you two talking about?"

"I'm just messing with Daren about this girl he brought back here."

"Mmm hmm," Amanda said looking at Daren.

"What, why you looking at me for?"

Amanda had seen the whole thing so he didn't know what to say.

He searched in his head for a few seconds.

"Whatever, I don't know why you're Mmm hmm-ing me," was the best he came up with.

"We gotta talk ," Amanda said still looking at Daren accusingly.

"Alliyah gets back today right?" Maurice wanted to break the tension.

"Yeah, her grandmother said she would drop her off at about three but you know what that means."

"Five," they both said in unison.

Daren smiled at how much they had grown into almost one person.

"How was your evening?"

Amanda paused for a second and imagined Max's steely hard dick sliding slowly into her.

"I was just here, watching TV, getting some me time."

She did not feel any guilt about cheating on Maurice. As far as she knew he had cheated on her a million times. He had cheated her out of her entire twenties and all he ever wanted to do was hang with his boys. She had desires, she had wants, and since he was too busy she needed to handle her business. Plus it was not like she searched out Max; it all got started by accident.

Chapter Seventeen

Brenton walked sluggishly down Lafayette
toward his apartment, he lived at 139 Emerson, in a
penthouse apartment with a sweeping vista. From
his roof he had a three hundred and sixty degree
view of all of Brooklyn plus the Manhattan skyline.
In the summers his roof was *the place* for parties.
There is something magical about being on a roof
in Brooklyn watching the sun set over Manhattan.

  His head was still a little foggy. His mouth dry
and talc-like, he needed some liquids, but there
were no stores close by. He struggled on. Then all
of a sudden he felt a switch fly inside his body. It
was like his sixth sense got turned on. It was as if
he was bitten by a sensory bug, his skin prickled.
The hairs on the back of his neck stood up. Was he
about to faint? For a second he thought he was, but
then he looked back. And there in the sunlight
jogging toward him was this figure, this person
wearing a silhouette of light.

  He was fully awake now. Brenton had no idea
who she was but for some strange reason he felt
something. What that thing was he could not

describe. But it was something he was not familiar with. She moved something inside of him. As she got closer he knew exactly what it was.

"Ah," he tried to get her attention and for the first time he could not find the words.

But she must have felt him too because as she passed him she slowed then stopped about ten paces ahead of him. She turned and they were both frozen in a bubble of their own. She pointed at him. And *Bang*. He was under her spell.

"Where do I know you from?" she asked narrowing her eyes.

The old Brenton kicked back in. "I was about to say the same thing, have we met before?" he said walking toward her like a deal maker.

"I am sure we have, I'm Emily, Emily Dangerfield." There was an evil glint in her eye.

"Mm Dangerfield, I like the sound of that."

"Now do you?"

"Mrs. Emily Dangerfield right?" He toyed with her.

"No, just Emily Dangerfield, but if you want to change that, that could be arranged," she said with a knowing smile on her face.

"Ooooh," Brenton said looking her up and down. "I like the sound of that."

Her form fitting spandex left nothing to the imagination. For a second there Brenton was nervous. She looked him up and down while playfully walking around him surveying his parts.

"So what's your name Mr. I like the sound of that?"

Brenton was sure he had met his match. He smiled. She was fit and limber and pliable. He already saw them together in bed; he had a quick flash of himself giving it to her in the shower.

"Brenton Allen," he took her hand.

"Brenton Allen, why do I know that name?" She looked at him closely.

"I don't know, time travel maybe, I went to the past and introduced myself to you so that when you met me today you would feel like we knew each other."

She gave him the *oh really* face but his idea was pretty amusing so she smiled.

"Well I have to finish my run." She turned to leave, this was a part of her game, she was only checking to see if he was going to let her leave.

Brenton held on to her hand. "I think we should definitely exchange numbers," he said in his best Black James Bond voice.

"Should we?" she said as she pulled her hand out of his and walked a few paces away.

She knew he was watching her ass roll. She was a master. If she was a painter she would be Salvador Dali. Brenton's heart stopped in his chest. He had wanted many women in his life but none the way he wanted Emily right now.

She stopped and bent over showing off her flexibility. She almost touched her forehead onto her knee as she reached into a secret pocket close to the ankle of her spandex pants and pulled out a card. She looked back at Brenton through her legs and thought to herself, *"New client? Or new lover?"* She was not sure, maybe both.

She turned and walked toward him throwing her hips from side to side as if she was in a movie. It was silly really, but in that moment for both of them it was perfect, it was right. She knew she had him. He knew he had her. She slipped the card gently into his hand. And *Bang*.

He was slipping his dick gently into her. She gasped for air, as his warm dick parted her on the inside. It seemed as if they had been transported from Lafayette Street straight onto Brenton's couch. Her spandex pants around one ankle as she straddled his lap and rode him slowly.

"Hold, hold, hold on one second," she barely got the words out.

"Shhhh, just-just-just keep, oh my God."

Brenton was in the pussy of a lifetime; who was this woman? She was moving so slow and with so much purpose that if his dick had Braille on it she would have been able to read it with her insides.

"One second, just one second I promise." She paused and picked up her phone. Fixed her hair and dialed.

Brenton could hear the phone ringing on the other side. A male voice picked up. She looked directly into Brenton's eyes as she placed her finger on her lips.

"Hey honey I am out jogging right now and I see this," she looked Brenton up and down, "this sweet little thing and I was wondering if I could…"

"Go ahead," the voice stated nonchalantly. "See you later, I think I may go visit Keisha, is that cool?"

"Of course, tell her I said hi, see you soon, love you."

The voice on the other end said, "Love you too babe."

Brenton's dick got harder when he realized what was happening. He was inside this woman and she was on the phone with her boyfriend telling him she was going to fuck him. But Brenton needed confirmation.

"Was that your boyfriend?"

"Yeah, I had to tell him."

"Who are…"

"Shhh…" She cut him off, leaned in then whispered in his ear. "Just shut up and fuck me, fuck me real good."

Chapter Eighteen

 B y mid-afternoon Sophie was bored. Max was passed out on the couch. He was nursing a slight headache. He had all the blinds closed. She did not want to disturb him. Her mind ran on Meghan. She paused for a moment and took a deep breath as she decided to call.

"Hey Sophie how are you?" Meghan was a little hesitant. She and Sophie had not spoken about what had happened at Outpost. They had spoken a few times since but avoided the issue.

"What are you doing today? We should hang out, talk, and by the way thank you so, so much for recommending that therapist." Sophie sounded happy and free, not like her regular controlled self.

"She's amazing right?" Meghan said enthusiastically.

"She is so honest about everything; you will not believe how much she has helped." Sophie chimed back in.

"Let's go to Outpost for brunch," Meghan said in a soft tone.

"Outpost… hmmm…" Sophie was flirting uncontrollably.

They both had the same thought at the same time but they both put it out of their heads in the same instant. Meghan closed her eyes to recall the sweet smell of Sophie.

"How about you come over here and I'll make you brunch," Meghan had a slight tone of authority in her voice.

The subtle command in Meghan's voice turned Sophie on. Sophie knew exactly what that authority meant.

"When do you want me to come?" Sophie said softly.

"Come now, I just got up, I am about to jump in the shower, the door will be open."

Sophie thought to herself, *"LORD."* She fainted a little in her chest. Her poor little heart started beating really fast. That first encounter had happened to a more reserved Sophie. She started plotting in her head exactly what was going to happen the moment she got to Meghan's place.

Brenton was sprawled out on his couch. Emily was still sitting on his dick with her body falling over to the side. They had both been exhausted, him from drinking the night before and her from running earlier. It was almost 1pm.

"Shit!" He jumped to his feet; throwing off Emily's legs as he stood up.

His dick slid out of the condom and the liquid inside spilled onto the floor. The condom was still half way inside of her. Still partly asleep she pulled the rest out and plopped it on the floor. Brenton was hurrying to get his clothes on while trying to find paper towels to clean up the spill. He was supposed to meet KEV at Pillow on Myrtle at 12:30pm, he had totally forgotten. He was dressed and ready to go in a few minutes.

"I'll be back in a few," he said as he was about to go out the door.

"You leaving?"

"No, I just have to go meet this guy for like ten minutes at Pillow and I'll be back."

"Come here," her voice soaking with yearning.

Brenton's dick jumped in his pants as he heard her moan. She was not horny, after all they had just fucked to exhaustion, but she wanted to prove to herself that she was the boss.

As he walked back to her from the door she spread her legs open and started rubbing her clit gently. Her eyes still closed.

"Come here." She pointed to a spot on the floor.

He stood in the spot. He was standing next to her face. Her moaning was animated now. Somehow she was able to unzip his pants with her teeth and reach into his pants with her tongue and started sucking his dick. Her mouth on his dick wiped his mind clean of his meeting.

Sophie walked into Meghan's apartment carefully. She could hear the shower running.

"Hey Sophie I'll be out soon, have a seat, there is freshly brewed coffee in the pot if you want."

"Ok," Sophie replied.

She made herself a cup of coffee and sat on the couch and waited for Meghan.

What are you doing here Sophie, why are you trying to hook up with your best friend? What kind of a person are you? Ok, ok calm down and stop judging yourself. We will just have brunch, sit and chat like we always do, just like old times. This is what Sophie was saying to herself when Meghan walked out of the shower. What Sophie did not know was that Meghan had planned this whole thing out. Sophie didn't realize that there was no brunch in the kitchen or on the table.

When Meghan walked out with all that steam coming off her goose pimpled flesh it hit Sophie. *"This bitch!"* She smiled, Meghan had never been afraid to go after what she wanted. She walked over to Sophie and stood in front of her. Sophie quietly placed her cup on the floor and slinked into the couch. Meghan removed her towel and mounted Sophie slowly.

Twenty minutes later and Emily's ankles were next to her ears while Brenton was grunting his way to a full bodied orgasm. She felt the semen as it shot out of him and sent a shiver through her body.

She knew it then. She had him. She smiled softly as she patted his head and rubbed his back. Brenton had once again forgotten that KEV was waiting for him at Pillow.

His phone rang. It was KEV.

Brenton mumbled in to the phone. "One second. I'll be there in like five minutes I am just up the street, see you soon."

"Whatever nigga," KEV hissed without an ounce of care in the world.

Brenton hurried out the door.

Sophie was on the bottom of a 69 looking up at Meghan's juicy pussy. Meghan had been licking and nibbling at Sophie's clit for a few minutes now and the more she licked and sucked the wetter Sophie got. Sophie took her first mouth full of Meghan's vagina and knew intuitively what to do. She did not particularly know exactly what to do but she knew what might feel good. So she pulled Meghan's ass all the way down onto her face and went to work.

She pressed her tongue into her as deep as she could. And she licked and slurped and nibbled and kissed and fingered and stayed at it until she could feel Meghan trembling while her insides tightened. Meghan came a few times, one big one then about five small ones. Sophie could not touch her for a while. They lay next to each other with not much to say.

"So what are we doing?" Meghan asked hesitantly.

"I, I, I have no idea Meg." Sohpie thought about Max. She smiled for a moment. *"Maybe they could have a threesome. Nah, it would be weird."*

"I think we should definitely not do this again, I mean I totally love you Sophie, you know, like, like a sister. Not like a sister-sister cause that would be gross. But I love you Sophie and it seems like this is going to destroy our friendship."

Meghan turned toward Sophie. Sophie kept looking up at the ceiling.

"I don't think it will."

Meghan did not agree. "Eventually our feelings will get in the way Sophie, plus you are engaged, what about Max? What would Max think?"

"Max, Max I think he would probably be into something like this," Sophie said as she turned toward Meghan. "We have been friends for so long, I can't see us not being friends."

"I know, but sometimes…" Megan wanted to continue but Sophie caught her mouth with her lips. They kissed for a while then lay in each other's arms for the rest of the afternoon.

Chapter Nineteen

"How was L.A brah?" Brenton greeted KEV as he walked in.

"Shit was hot man, them dudes out there show a nigga love though, know I'm saying."

"Shit that's what we need man, that's that return money, they gon' be begging to have you back. I give it like two weeks they'll be calling, bet."

"Man the bitches out there are on it too man."

"I thought your wife went with you?" Brenton asked.

"She did, but you know how we do right?" KEV was as cool as a cucumber.

He was not particularly ugly but he definitely did not get any points for looks. All his bravado and swag came from his self-belief. KEV's wife was damn near a super model. In any other life time KEV marrying Julia would have been a genetic and statistical impossibility.

"She be watching the dick hard man." He shook his head in disappointment. "But niggas gon' be niggas right?"

Breton kind of smiled. The question did not need answering. Brenton thought about Emily, Ms. Dangerfield. He shook his head from side to side.

"So what's the deal man?" KEV wanted to get down to business.

"Got this cat out of the UK wanted to do five shows. Originally he was saying one show for like fifty. I was like no I need more than fifty for KEV and he was like what if I can get you five shows could you do fifty. I was like nah, I need sixty; he was all like blah blah blah and I was like yow, call me when you wanna do business and hung up." Brenton said all this in like nine seconds.

KEV almost jumped out of his seat. "Nigga I just did a show in L.A. for twenty grand and you turn down a nigga who is offering fifty? Plus it's in the UK!"

Brenton was smiling. "Yow KEV, I got this, so dude calls me back in like five seconds right? We got five shows in the UK, $300, 000."

KEV was frozen. "You ain't fucking with me right?"

"Nah man, what the fuck kinda nigga you think I am. I do not jokes about the bread, ok." Brenton sat back.

He was pretty proud of how far he and KEV had come.

KEV stood up in all his hip hop glory, his shades, his Gucci belt, his v-neck white tee, his gold fronts, the Yankee fitted, his colorful Jordans and his almost skinny jeans and said, "Gimme some fucking love nigga."

It was as if the Albany projects were flashing through his head. All KEV could think was, *"$300,000."*

"Let me buy you a drink nigga, a sandwich something." He wanted to show gratitude.

The last thing Brenton wanted to do was have a drink or a sandwich.

Brenton changed gears in about zero seconds and speaking at the speed of light he said, "So listen, I got this sweet ass fuckin' girl waiting for me totally naked in my bed and I would really love to have a drink with you but guess what? Never keep a naked woman waiting."

And with that, *Bang*, he was out the door.

Chapter Twenty

As soon as he stepped out of Pillow his phone rang. It was Max. Brenton ignored the call. He was heading back to Emily. His phone rang again. It was Max again.

"Yow" Brenton answered.

"You good?" Max rasped into the phone.

"Yeah I'm good." Brenton was speed walking while he spoke.

"Man I am done man, I am fuckin' done drinking. My fucking head is killing me, my kidneys hurt, my entire body is feeling all retarded and shit. If you ever see me say I'm gonna drink again I need you to fucking shoot me bro."

"Done?" Brenton laughed as he answered.

This was vintage Max. He quits drinking every weekend only to forget that he did the following weekend.

"So, what happened with those two chicks man?"

"Those two chicks? Fuck those two chicks man, you need to see this girl I met today."

"Girl you met today? Badder than that Spanish chick you left with last night?"

"Yow, Max fuck the Spanish chick man, when I say this girl is bad, man, she is ridiculous, I think she may be the one bro." Brenton sounded a note that Max had never heard before.

Brenton was never into taking women seriously. For him it was always a game, it was just for play and he was always, just, playing. For him relationships were never serious.

"Brent, you ok man?" Max asked in a hoarse dumbfounded voice.

"What do you mean?" Brenton sounded clueless.

"Dude, you just said this girl may be the one."

"No I didn't?" Brenton thought back to what he had said.

He was not sure. He knew himself and he knew he would have never said anything like that. Maybe his mind was still a little foggy and he slipped.

"You kinda did B." Max was certain.

"Nah, never that." Brenton knew deep down how he felt about Emily but he had a reputation to uphold. "What do I look like saying some girl I just met is the one, you crazy, hell fuckin' no." He was only convincing himself at this point. He got on the elevator in his building. "Yow Max listen let's catch up later, I am on the eleva…" His phone went dead. "Fuck it." He hung up.

Brenton could not wait until the elevator stopped on his floor. He was nervous for no reason. This was very much unlike Brenton. For a second he had to stop and ask himself, *"What the fuck Brenton? This ain't you."*

As soon as he opened his door his heart was at peace. Emily was still on his couch sleeping, or was she? She was lying with her ass hoisted in such a perfect position that she had to have planned it. He bit into his bottom lip and stood in the doorway and admired her. She was beautiful. Her body was perfect. She was smart. She was witty. And most of all she knew she was all of those things.

Brenton walked over slowly and kissed her on her cheek. She felt so familiar. It was almost impossible that he had just met her a few hours ago. Emily knew the moment he placed his key in the door. Her position was not some random act but she knew how to pretend as if it was random. She liked Brenton and depending on how he played his cards maybe they could be long term lovers. She wanted someone who was open to her sexuality, someone who was willing to play. She hated the clingy types. In her heart she was praying he would not get clingy.

"How was your meeting?"

"It was amazing," he whispered as he unbuckled his belt.

It seems he could not get enough of her. He slipped his pants off. He held his dick in his hand and looked at her on her stomach with her ass hoisted just so. In his mind he wanted to enter her raw. Would she let him? He did not know but why not try right?

He nibbled on her ear and passed his teeth along the nape of her neck she gyrated upward towards him. That was his signal. *"She wanted it,"* he thought to himself. And just as he was about to plunge himself into her she clapped her hand flush over her vagina.

"Uh uhm, get a condom," she muffled softly.

He was a little heartbroken but then again she did the right thing. He went into his bed room and got a condom but all he could think of was how amazing her pussy must feel raw. It was beyond real with the condom but *Jesus* he could only imagine how much better it would be without.

By the time he got back she was wide awake on all fours waiting for him. He slid up behind her and she pressed back against him and gyrated a slow prayer into his lap. He held onto her hips, held on for dear life. She pushed back against him gently then looked over her shoulder and requested his tongue. They kissed as she gyrated and pushed back against his thick firm dick. She loved the width, loved the fact that she had to push back real hard to get the whole thing in. He wet his fingers in his mouth and reached around and started massaging her clit.

"Ooooh, you know what you are doing."

"Not really, I'm just doing what you want me to do."

"Ok, since you're doing what I want you to do, how about you fuck me like you mean it."

"What?"

"Was this a challenge?" Brenton thought to himself.

"Come on you heard me." She said all this while they were kissing.

"Really, that's what you want?" Brenton got a little firmer with her and grabbed her hips a little tighter.

"Yeah, I like that, go ahead daddy."

She loved talking dirty. But she knew she had to take it easy with Brenton she did not want to spoil him just yet. But his stroke was getting beautiful. She was somewhere between schooling him and getting schooled. Brenton had taken her challenge as a threat to his manhood and she was enjoying every moment of it. She knew exactly how to motivate her lovers. She knew what buttons to push to get the results she wanted.

"Oh, my god, why are you playing with me, Brenton?"

"Really, you think this is playing?"

"I need you to treat me like a grown ass woman, ok."

He clicked into third. This was his power stroke. Slow and firm. She loved it.

"Oh yes, now we're getting somewhere," she screamed back at him as he pulled on her hair and held her head in an awkward position.

Her pussy felt so good that Brenton had to check to make sure the condom was still on. A warm feeling started building at the root of his dick and slowly climbed up into his stomach. And the faster he stroked the warmer the feeling became and the wetter she got. Emily kept up a steady dose of shit talking. By this time Brenton had her face mushed up against a pillow and her ass in the air. *"Slow down Brenton,"* he said to himself. And *Bang.*

The real Brenton showed up. Yep. He was in charge. She kept pushing back against him hard and fast. He knew her orgasm was building. He was gonna give her one but he would make her beg for it. And beg she did. She wanted it hard and fast, he decided against it and gave it to her firm and slow. And when he felt her tightening up around his dick he gave it to her with a vengeance and she called him, "Oh God!" as she came.

Brenton was covered in sweat. He had not come but he was very happy on the inside watching Emily going through her aftershocks.

"Did you come?" she said out of breath.

"Nah, it's ok though," he said nonchalantly. "It's not about me coming. I just wanna make sure you do." He had a sly smile on his face.

Emily was impressed. She turned around and tore the condom off his dick to return the favor.

And when he shot his creamy semen all over her breasts she said, "Well there, I wanna make sure you come too, ok."

They took a short break and within fifteen minutes they were at it again. Nothing can ever come close to the passion between two people who are just introducing themselves to each other. By 7pm they were totally dehydrated. Emily dragged herself out of Brenton's bed, took a shower and went home to her boyfriend.

Brenton laid in bed going over the words to Ice Cube's *Today was a good day*. He wanted to ask her when he would see her again but he decided against it.

Chapter Twenty One

"Let's do lunch tomorrow." A text landed on Max's phone. It was Amanda.

"Where?" Max replied.

He did not want to meet her but he knew he had to sort out the details of their ongoing rendezvous. The first time it happened he felt bad and he hated himself for it, but by the third time he knew he was a bastard. It was not like she was forcing herself on him. He could have said no.

"Meet me at the diner at Atlantic and Third."

"What time?"

"12:30."

Max wondered what Amanda had up her sleeve. For a moment he really wanted to know but then he thought about his boy Maurice. *"Damn, what kind of a person am I?"* he thought to himself. Then he had a weird thought. *"Better me than some strange dude."* It was a sad state of affairs. He decided that he would go but he would not fall for her shenanigans. He was going to put an end to this whole thing.

Amanda was upstairs in her bed as she texted Max. Maurice was downstairs watching golf with Daren. Daren seemed bored.

"So fo' real Daren, what's up with you?"

"What do you mean?"

"Come on man, you know what I mean."

Amanda sent Max another text. *"Panties or no panties?"*

Max wanted no part of it. *"I don't care."*

Amanda took that as a welcome. If she was in a different mood she would have noticed that he said, *"I DON'T CARE."*

His response seemed promising to her. She got up from her bed, locked the door, went into her underwear drawer and took out her favorite vibrating dildo. Her dildo collection had become her best friend for a little over a year. It became her best friend when Maurice stopped having sex with her.

Daren looked at Maurice with disgust. He knew exactly what Maurice was asking him.

"No, I do not know what you mean."

"I mean, you are gay right?"

"Yes, I'm gay." If he could have murdered Maurice with his eyes Maurice would be a dead man.

"So what was that with the girl?"

"It was nothing, we were just dancing right?"

"It was a little more than dancing, you took her back here."

121

"I know we were just hanging out."

Maurice gave him the side eye.

Daren was attempting to be honest. "Well I don't know how to describe it but whenever I get drunk, like really drunk I feel a little bit attracted to women. It's kinda weird."

"So does that mean you're bi?"

"No, I'm not bi, not at all, ah huh, not me."

"Why are you not bi though?"

"Because, I don't like girls like that."

"But you just said when you are drunk…"

"Yeah but when I am sober, I would never, NEVER touch one of those bitches."

Amanda removed her underwear and lay on her back with her knees thrown to the sides. She clicked the vibrator on. The sound of the hum hardened her clit. She passed her tongue across the tip of the silicon penis and pretended it was Max's. She took it fully into her mouth, closed her eyes, and played with it with her tongue. Her pussy overflowed with juices. By the time she slid the vibrator across her clit she was already so wet it took zero effort to slide the entire thing inside. She pulled it out and marveled at how creamy it was.

Recently she noticed that her sex drive had about quadrupled. All she thought about was sex or getting fucked. And there she was living with her husband who refused to have sex with her; sometimes she thought he may even have scorned her.

She gently rammed the motorized penis back inside herself and coiled as the vibrations shook her from the inside. She then pressed the tickler against her clit and rode the waves of vibrations until she was stuttering Max's name.

Maurice was not happy with Daren's explanation but for now he would let it go.

"You gotta be careful out there man. You never know how your actions could affect people."

"I am fine, ok." He was certain there was no harm done.

"Ok, if you say so." Maurice said knowingly.

Chapter Twenty Two

Max sat up on his couch. His brain was buzzing.
Hangovers were not his thing. He walked slowly to
the fridge, got a pitcher of water and took it to the
head. He walked back to the couch and sat down,
turned the television on hoping something really
boring could put him out of his misery.

Everything seemed dreamy; he could not tell if he
was asleep or awake. There was a knock at his
door. *"Who the hell could this be?"* He got up to
check the door. He was wearing a pair of white
jockey shorts. The only person he was expecting
was Sophie, she should be heading home by this
time but she had her keys so who could it be?

He checked through the peep hole. It was
Vanessa. He opened the door.

"Vanessa, what are you doing here?"

She pushed passed him without a word.

"Listen, Vanessa, Sophie is on her way back and
this is not the time, how did you get here?"

They were in his bedroom. Her back was toward
him. Vanessa turned and looked him in the eyes
and he knew exactly why she came. Her lips were

so juicy. Sophie would be here any moment. Fuck. He definitely couldn't do anything to fuck up his relationship now.

"Listen, Vanessa." He tried to make his case but before he could get another word out she grabbed the nape of his neck. And *Bang*.

It was as if he had totally forgotten that Sophie would be on her way home.

"Shut up and fuck me Max." She stuck her tongue in his mouth.

"But, but Sophie will be here any mo- mo- moment." He was beginning to lose his battle against her.

She chucked him onto the bed and tore his jockey's off of him. Grabbed his dick and licked it hard and slow while looking him dead in the eyes.

"Does Sophie suck your dick like this, huh Max?" She had her seductive gait on.

"Ok, ok, ok we can fuck but we have to hurry, I can't fuckin' believe I am doing this."

He knew from the look in her eye that she would not leave unless he fucked her. So he bent her over and fucked her as hard and as fast as he could. Luckily, she was so horny that she came almost as soon as he entered her. By the time he came three whole minutes had passed.

"Can I use your bathroom?"

He looked at her as if she was crazy. "Vanessa, I am not sure you understand, Sophie is about to be here any moment now."

"Really? I can barely tell…"

She walked past him nonchalantly and went toward his bathroom.

He got his clothes on and stood by the front door with the door slightly ajar. The pipe was running in the bathroom. He heard the toilet flush. *"Thank God,"* he thought to himself. He saw the elevator numbers moving to the first floor. *"Shit, I hope that's not Sophie,"* he started panicking. He knocked on the bathroom door.

"I'm done, I'm coming, damn, what's the hurry?"

"Sophie is on the first floor!"

"Ok, I get, I get it."

She hurried out the bathroom and gave him a long hard kiss at the door. She saw the elevator numbers moving up and looked at Max. She loved to make him sweat. She smiled.

"I'll take the stairs."

"Thank you so much."

As soon as the door to the stairs closed the elevator door opened and Sophie stepped off. By this time Max was back on the couch pretending to sleep. A text message landed on his phone. He heard Sophie jangling her keys in the key hole. The message said, *"Thank you. I needed that."*

Max was fuming, he was so mad he refused to respond.

"I was in the neighborhood and I just wanted to say hi, we should definitely hang out soon, maybe meet at the Brooklyn Moon, wink, lol."

Sophie came in, she was spritely. "Hey babe, how was your..? Never mind."

She saw that he was still in the darkness sleeping. She walked over, gave him a kiss on the cheek and sat next to him and rubbed his back. Max was still shaking inside. Sophie sat there a watched him sleep for a long while.

Chapter Twenty Three

Brenton's phone rang. He was at Habana Outpost. It was around 1pm. Normally he would have one eye on his work and the other on the women who herded themselves into Habana, but today no such thing. All he could think of was Emily. Her scent haunted him all day like she was trapped in his head.

"Yes." He answered on the last possible ring.

"Yow Brent." The voice on the other side sounded happy.

"Oh shit Trace." Brenton was glad to hear Trace's voice.

Trace was his cousin from London. They had both left Jamaica around the same time in their teens. They came to New York with their families to live but about ten years ago Trace moved to London for work. Trace was four years older than Brenton. Trace was Brenton's favorite cousin; actually Brenton followed him to Syracuse for college. Side by side they could have been twins. Trace was the only person Brenton considered a superior. Trace invented everything Brenton knew about life.

"I'm gonna be in New York next weekend bruv, you gonna be around?" He had a slight hint of an English accent mixed in with his old island accent topped off with a little bit of Brooklyn. He was the real Black James Bond.

"When, where, dude you have to stay with me, I got this new crib, oh wait till you see the new crib."

"I'll be coming in to JFK on Thursday 6:00pm Delta flight 1027."

"Delta, flight 1027, 6pm." Brenton wrote down the information.

For the first time today he was not thinking about Emily. As soon as he got off the phone Brenton started texting his friends inviting them to his next party. He was planning a party to celebrate KEV's overseas trip but now it would definitely be for his cousin's homecoming. He was alive again. *"Fuck sweating this girl,"* he thought to himself. He looked at his phone. Should he call her? He found her number and just as he was about to hit call, here comes the redhead.

At this point he was sure she was stalking him. She sat down across from him with her laptop and some granola looking tote bag that she carried around like a hipster medal of honor.

"Hey Brenton." She wanted something or maybe she didn't but she was very friendly.

"Hey, how are you?" They exchanged kisses.

"On the cheek, on the cheek," Brenton said in his head as she reached in. This was no place for all that fancy-schmancy.

"So, you left so early yesterday."

"I had some things to take care of, had a meeting with KEV, this rapper I work with."

"KEV! Get out of here you know KEV?"

"Do I know KEV? I am his booking agent."

"Really?"

"Yes really."

"I love his music!" She started singing. "All these bitches wanna love on KEV, stop. All these bitches wanna love on KEV, stop… Oh my god he is my fav!"

She had just gone from Hamptons socialite to hood-rat in less than three seconds. Brenton gave her the side eye and the grimace face. She saw the look.

"What, you don't love KEV?"

"That's my dude, I am his booking agent, of course I love him." He tried to calm her down. He liked her as a hipster more than he liked her as a hood-rat.

"So what do you do, how do you know about KEV?"

He'd rather talk about what she did than about KEV or her forays into hood-rattery.

"I'm a writer."

"What do you write?"

"Fader, I'm freelance, but I mostly write for Fader Magazine, oh my God…" she said calmly as if she just got a revelation from the top of the mountain. "I should do a story about KEV."

"Hmm," Brenton said acting as if he was not interested though he knew a story in Fader would definitely change KEV's career.

"Can you…?" She paused. "Don't take this the wrong way or anything but, can you introduce me to him or his manager?"

"Well one, I can't introduce you to his manager because his manager is his wife and she don't like KEV having white bitches around him." Her face fell apart. That's when he chimed back in. "Just kidding, I can introduce you to him, hold on a second."

Brenton took out his phone, hit dial and put his phone on speaker. The phone rang twice.

"Yow B," KEV sounded comatose.

"I got this young lady," he looked at the redhead with an assuring glance, "who wants to meet you. She wants to do an article on you in Fader Magazine."

"Fader?" KEV had no clue.

"Yeah, Fader." Brenton wanted him to play along.

"What the fuck is Fader? Niggas from the hood don't read Fader."

Brenton gave the redhead another reassuring look.

"Yeah, yeah I get that but you see all them hipster kids in Williamsburg who be at your shows. They do. And this is just a doorway to them man. They wanna feel like they know you, you gotta drop all that hood shit man. The bread is not gonna come from the hood. It's those same hipster kids that read Fader that will go on iTunes and buy the entire album, not just a track." Brenton said all this in about five seconds.

"Fuck it, tell that bitch we can do it."

KEV did not sound as if he cared either way; he was just going along with whatever was going to make money. Brenton gave her a wink and the *white harambe* sign.

She returned it with an enthusiastic, "Yes!"

"So, how about we meet with her this evening so I can introduce you to her."

"Where?"

"Cornerstone."

"Bet, what time?"

Brenton looked at the redhead. "Eight o'clock?"

"Cool, let me get back to this blunt man."

KEV was perpetually high, but somehow he was able to function like a normal person.

"Remember man, eight o'clock," Brenton reiterated.

"I got it, I got it," and with that KEV hung up.

"No fuckin' way," the redhead was psyched.

"How long have you known him?"

"Let's just say I knew him before he was KEV, I knew him when he was," and they said it in unison, "K-Paper."

Brenton gave her an approving look. "You really know your stuff."

"When I said I love KEV, I really mean I love K-E-V!" She was dead serious.

Brenton did not know how to digest what she just said. He narrowed his eyes and looked at her closely.

"I gotta watch you!" he said. They both laughed.

"Guess who left this morning? Maria." She asked and answered her own question.

"I hope she had a fun-filled weekend." They both smiled. "Do you have any of the articles you wrote at your apartment? I would love to check a few out." Brenton had finally found a way to get her name.

"I've got plenty." Her mood seemed to change. "Guess who left something for you? Maria."

"What did she leave?" Brenton was puzzled, what could Maria have left?

The redhead leaned over the table and whispered, "A blowjob."

And Bang. She stood up, slid her laptop into her tote bag and walked off, her hipster sundress blowing in the light breeze.

Brenton's mouth was agape. "What the fuck?"

This girl was truly a work of art. His dick slowly started rising in his pants. It was not what she said

133

that turned him on; he was turned on by the sheer amount of balls it took to pull that off.

"You coming to get it or what?" She had a naughty tone in her voice.

"I'll be there in two seconds." Brenton called out to the waiter. "Waiter!"

Brenton checked his watch. It was 2pm. He had to get some work done but fuck it. This girl was gonna get Emily out of his head.

The redhead had his dick in her mouth the moment the elevator doors closed. 3pm they were both on their backs on her Ikea sheets panting like dogs.

"You have anything to drink?" Brenton needed some liquids.

"Sure." She rushed off then came back with two bottles of hipster beer.

"So this is how it's gonna be, huh?"

"What do you mean?" she asked biting into her bottom lip; she was ready for another round.

"You just gonna fuck me and feed me beer, is that it?" Brenton realized that he was beginning to like…, "*What the fuck was her name?*"

"Well, that and celery, I got celery!"

She ran off to the kitchen and came back with four huge stalks of celery and a clump of what looked like chunky raw peanut butter and a bottle of honey.

Brenton had one question. "What's the honey for?" She smiled. And *Bang*.

Chapter Twenty Four

Sophie walked into the office of Ms. Clearmont. She was a little disheveled when Sophie walked in. She cleared her throat when she saw Sophie.

"Who was that young man I saw in the hall way? Was that your son?"

"Looks like he could be, right?"

But the truth is he wasn't her son and he wasn't there to change the ink cartridge in the copier. Ms. Clearmont straightened her skirt suit and sat down.

"I know I look up there in age but I have no children," she said looking over the top of her spectacles trying to look formal; but her eyes were smiling.

"I'm so sorry, that's not what I meant." Sophie realized how awkward her statement may have sounded.

Ms. Clearmont's office was not the typical therapist's office. It was more like a hookah lounge without the hookahs. Yes, she had the therapy couch but it looked like that couch was for her personal use.

"So tell me how are things progressing?" She went into therapy mode.

"Well with regard to Max, well?" Sophie paused.

"Yeah, go on."

"Things are so, so, so different than they used to be. I know it's been like a week, but that whole dressing up thing has really changed everything."

"What do you mean?"

"It's strange, whenever I get dressed up it's like I am a different person."

"What do you mean a different person?" This sounded intriguing to Ms. Clearmont.

"Well, when I get dressed up it is almost as if I become someone else, it's as if I am not Sophie anymore. And I feel free and I can talk dirty and act dominant and be in charge of my sexuality."

"Isn't that what you wanted, to be freer?"

"Yes, but when I am Sophie I can't find that person, when I am not dressed up I am just boring old me."

"No, no, no, the dressed up person and the regular person are the same, you have just hidden one of them for so long you do not know how to access her fully, as of yet. Just give her room to come out."

Sophie was quiet for a while processing what she had just heard.

"Ok, ok, ok," Sophie said tapping the side of her forehead. "Also for some reason all I can think about now is having sex. Before, sex was just something you did because you were an adult but now I feel this drive, this desire to just have sex all the time and it all started when…" Sophie paused, "Ok, ok so remember when I said I can only be all sexy and forceful and all that when I am dressed up?"

"Yes."

"Well that was not all true."

"Hmm." Ms. Clearmont leaned forward.

Sophie leaned forward also and lowered her voice. "Well I was at a friend of mine's house the other day and, and…" Sophie looked down at her hands. Her hands were shaking. "And she came out of the shower and, and instantly, actually even before I went to her house I was thinking about it but as soon as she came out of the bathroom I just had this whole feeling, the way I feel when I am dressed up just came over me."

"And why do you think that happened?"

"I am not sure." Sophie's brain was reaching for answers.

Ms. Clearmont reached across her desk and touched Sophie's trembling hands. Sophie looked up. And *Bang*. They both knew it. They were both frozen for a few seconds.

"Well I have to get back to work," Sophie said nervously and with that she was out the door in a flash.

Ms. Clearmont was glad Sophie left because she was not sure she was willing to put her professional integrity to the test. She looked over at her old copier and thought, yep, the copier needs more ink.

Chapter Twenty Five

"**I** think we should stop," Max said emotionless.

"Really, why?" Amanda thought this was a part of the game.

"Because you are married to my best friend Amanda." Max looked around the diner. It was deserted. This diner was always empty, how it stayed open God alone knew. "Maurice would fuckin' kill both of us if he found out."

"That's what makes it fun." She smiled and licked her lips.

She had perfect skin, beautiful teeth and eyes that said fuck me, fuck me, fuck me. Max thought about Sophie and how much their relationship was changing. He realized in that moment that Amanda was more of a threat to what he had with Sophie than his friendship with Maurice. Yes Maurice was his boy but if it came down to it he could do without Maurice but he loved Sophie. He loved her so much he stayed with her for years even when the sex was terrible. And now that the sex was amazing he was not trying to fuck it up.

"So, I went with option number two," she said as she paged through the menu.

"What is option number two?" He was totally confused.

She smiled. "No panties."

Max took a deep breath. "Listen, I am so serious, we should stop."

"I am serious too, I have no panties on and my pussy is crying out for you."

Max thought about Amanda bent over on her couch. That image would never leave his mind for the rest of his life, he was sure.

"We don't have to fuck; if you want I can just suck your dick." Her mouth watered as she said it, she bit into her bottom lip and narrowed her eyes.

Most men could walk away from sex, but a blow job is almost impossible to walk away from. Ask Clinton. Max held his face in his hands and took an even deeper breath.

"I can't do this, Maurice is my boy."

"Maurice is your boy? Maurice is your boy right? You think if the tables were turned Maurice would think twice about fucking *your* wife," she said with a bit of annoyance in her voice.

"I know he wouldn't fuck my wife," Max said blankly.

"Well I am Maurice's wife and he does not have any problems fucking around on me." Amanda in that moment was at her loneliest.

Max saw her hurt masquerading as bravado. She was a nice girl. He liked her but this was a weird situation. They were silent for a few moments just looking at each other; her fuck me eyes were worth their weight in gold. And maybe it was the sound of the oldies piping through the cheap speakers, or the sound of the Spanish cooks chattering in the kitchen or the old fat waitress counting her tips, but something about the atmosphere and Amanda seemed so desperate. Her desperation was an aphrodisiac crawling through his loins. The moment he had the thought, she spotted it in his posture, the way he leaned back in the seat and looked at her. She smiled. And *Bang*. It was decided.

"I have to go to the bathroom to wash my hands, our food will be here soon, you should wash yours also," she said as she slid out from the banquet.

One minute later Max and Amanda were in the bathroom in the basement, her skirt pulled up around her waist and one leg atop the toilet bowl. The bathroom was dingy, the walls were thin, the floors were sticky with cleaning solvent, and the fake Picasso on the wall said it all, The Dog. A stick figure drawing of a dog, in context, this made for the perfect place to fuck one's best friend's wife during lunch.

She screamed in silence and he grunted as they came in unison. She pulled her skirt down, kissed him, dabbed the sweat off his forehead and they headed back upstairs. Max did not stay for lunch.

He gathered his things, looked at her with a sad smile and said, "That's it, I'm done." Then he walked out.

Amanda knew it was not over but she was not going to make him any wiser. About half a block away Max got a text. *"The day you stop fucking me is the day I tell Maurice and Sophie."* Max stopped in the middle of the sidewalk, the world slid by.

Chapter Twenty Six

Brenton and KEV were sitting at the bar on the second floor at Cornerstone. Cornerstone was a pretty trendy spot on the corner of Dekalb and Adelphi. The name had changed many, many, many, many times over the past ten years. Name changes aside, it was consistently one of the happening spots in Brooklyn. It felt like home in the upstairs lounge, with couches and small tables and minimal lighting to give it that sexy feel, plus the roof top patio was all the rave during the summers.

A video DJ was spinning hip hop and pop music. He noticed KEV when KEV and Brenton walked in so he decided to play every video KEV has ever made. It got to a point where the bartender, a baldheaded Mexican dude with a Taliban beard and a boyish smile, had to go tell him to stop because he was embarrassing himself.

"I hate niggas who suck dick," KEV said in reference to the DJ; KEV was never one for subtlety.

"Tell me about it," Brenton agreed.

They were having Hennessy straight. KEV liked his drinks straight. He never understood why people would put juice in alcohol and fuck up the taste.

"It's eight fifteen man, where this bitch at?" KEV did not know much about Fader so waiting for them was a difficult task.

"She's coming, don't worry man, she's coming." Brenton was certain she would be there soon. As soon as he got the words out his phone rang. "See that's her right now." He looked at KEV with the phone away from his ear. "Yeah, where are you? Oh you're downstairs? At Cornerstone? How long you been down there? Sorry, my bad, we are upstairs. Cool."

He took a sip from his drink. "Listen man this interview could be a big deal, a'ight."

"I'm cool as a fan man." KEV smelled like a pound of skunk. His eyes were blood red.

The redhead was making her way up the spiral staircase. Brenton spotted her. She was trailed by a young guy with a camera. She almost broke her neck stumbling over herself to get to KEV.

"Hey Brenton how are you doing, this is KEV I am guessing," she said nervously.

"KEV this is…" and before Brenton could say another word.

"Marla Sterling, so good to meet you I am a big fan of your work." She took his hand enthusiastically.

Brenton smiled at the way she was fawning, but mostly he was smiling because he finally knew her name, *Marla Sterling*.

She had just lost all journalistic integrity. There was no way she could do anything objective. Brenton felt a small twinge of jealousy, not that he would care if she wanted to fuck KEV, no, he was jealous because he was not getting her attention. He watched her as she flirted with KEV like a petulant school girl. KEV kicked in that Brooklyn charm like a true hustler and within a few minutes he had her eating out of his hand. He was truly living out the lyrics to one of his songs; *If the pussy is easy I'm gonna get it.*

Brenton sat by the bar while KEV and Marla sat on the couch talking about KEV's career and his upcoming project, *Ratchet Pussy*.

"So what is going to be first single?" Marla asked.

KEV smiled. "I think the first single gon' be, *I'm tired of Ratchet Pussy.*"

He laughed at the reaction on her face. Brenton covered his face in embarrassment, he was not always proud of KEV's type of music but he knew it sold, so who else to sell it but him, fuck it people loved it so why not? The young guy with the camera was snapping pictures from odd angles. KEV was basking in the glory, all the while playing as if it was nothing.

"So we know you grew up not too far from here in the Albany projects right? What, what would you say to a young kid in the projects who has dreams of becoming a rapper like you?" Marla hit at the gut of all of KEV's bravado.

Brenton turned all the way around; he wanted to hear what KEV had to say about this one. The wrong words and KEV's career could sink. Brenton tried to signal to him to be careful but KEV was in a zone.

He took a sip from his Hennessy, licked his lips, tilted his head to the side and said, "Fuck trying to be like KEV man, grow up and be like you, if you spend all your time trying to be like me who is gon' be you homie?"

Brenton's mouth hit the floor. All of KEV's hood bravado had given way to such a deep philosophical idea that it almost brought a tear to Brenton's eye. *"Damn,"* Brenton thought to himself. KEV took another sip from his drink. It was as if he had not even realized how profound his statement was.

Marla was busy scribbling on her note pad. As soon as she was finished writing what KEV had said, she knew she had hit a gem. She re-read the line and just like that her arms were covered in goose bumps. She looked up from her notepad and KEV had transformed into her new messiah. And *Bang*.

"Oh my fucking god, oh god, oh god. I can't believe I'm doing this." Marla was straddling KEV's lap on the leather chair in her bedroom, riding her way to a beautiful orgasm.

KEV's pants were around his ankles his shirt and hat and glasses were still on. He was totally powerless as Marla went for hers. He had gotten the heads up from Brenton that it was ok but his conscience was eating at him so he was not totally committed to the act. KEV loved sex but mostly he loved *head*, less commitment, less intimacy, at least on his part. He did not have to deal with the actual person while getting head. Head was like a donation, sex was like volunteering and he did not like volunteering, too much work. He did not have to leave his weed cloud to get head. He had gotten this way from being around lots and lots of groupies, groupies who were lined up after shows to go back to his hotel with him.

Marla was on her final stretch toward her orgasm when KEV said, "Stop, stop this shit is whack."

And just like that everything ended. He almost broke her heart. There she was doing her best and he was not even a little bit impressed.

"But I, I didn't get a chance to…" Marla tried to guilt KEV into continuing.

KEV had lost his erection. Marla realized what had happened. She attempted to go down on him but KEV pushed her away.

"I'm good, I'm good, I just got a lot on ma mind, know-am-sayin'." KEV seemed a little sad.

"But if you want we can just cuddle." She was trying to console him.

"Cuddle, what the fuck I look like?" KEV stepped back.

"Hold on, hold on," she whispered as she approached him with caution. "How about if you just sat here…" she slowly pushed him back onto the small leather chair, "and I just lay on the bed right here and you watch me masturbate."

KEV agreed. He reached into his pocket and pulled out a spliff and lit it. Marla lay on her bed on her back and masturbated while KEV watched her moan and writhe with pleasure. After she came they sat in her bedroom in total silence until she fell asleep.

Chapter Twenty Seven

Max walked all the way from the diner to his apartment on Myrtle and Washington. He had removed his suit jacket and walked all that way trying to figure a way out of this mess he found himself in. He texted Brenton.

"Yow let's catch up later."

Brenton hit him back. *"How about Cornerstone?"*

Max, *"What time?"*

Brenton, *"About nine, I'll be there with KEV."*

Max, *"Cool."*

When he got to his apartment it was close to Three O'clock. Max was planning to just shower and chill maybe watch some sports and then meet up with Brenton later. Sophie was supposed to be at work, so when he heard light moaning coming from their bedroom he did not know what to think.

He paused in the hallway to listen. All he heard were feminine moans. He was a little turned on but he was also a bit angry. Was Sophie cheating on him with a woman? He was not sure. He snuck up to the bedroom door and pushed it gently. When he peeked in he saw Sophie kneeling on the bed with Meghan on her back spread eagle in front of her. Meghan saw Max as he walked in.

"Uh oh." She had a look of delight on her face.

"What happened?" Sophie enquired looking up at Meghan.

"We have company," Meghan said cautiously pointing at the door.

Max walked in slowly. "What's going on here?"

Sophie looked back and smiled. She had panicked for a second, but then her alter ego kicked in.

"Hey honey, look what I planned for you, I was just getting her warmed up."

"Oh really?" Max was skeptical.

How would she have known he was going to be home early? But this was no time to talk about details.

Sophie grabbed him by his waistband and pulled him onto the bed. And *Bang.* They kissed. Meghan tore his shirt off. Sophie pushed him onto his back and mounted him. She slipped him into her soaking wet pussy and rode him slowly. Max could not believe what was happening. This is definitely not the Sophie he knew, that was a fact. Meghan straddled his chest while she made out with Sophie. He slowly wrapped his arms around her thighs and pulled her unto his face and explored her from the inside with his tongue. They were in numerous positions and parings, and licked and sucked and bit and squeezed everything that would cause sensation. It all came to a screaming, panting, moaning orgasmic end with Max behind Meghan and Meghan's two fingers hitting Sophie's g-spot while her tongue caressed her clit.

The strange part of it all was how normal everyone acted after the whole thing.

"So I guess this is a onetime proposition," Max said hoping he would hear different.

Sophie looked at Meghan. "Yeah, I think so."

Meghan made a sad face, but she understood. If it was not for Sophie's fast thinking this could have been the end of Sophie and Max. Meghan felt a pang in her chest. The pang she felt, she knew was love. She had fallen in love with Sophie and there was no denying it. Max had questions about Meghan and Sophie but he decided to keep them for later.

Chapter Twenty Eight

Maurice stopped by The Five spot before he went home. The Five Spot is a half a block from his house on Washington. The Five Spot is an old school southern-styled place. Everything in there is red or dark wood. When you walk in it is as if you are walking into an old seventies movie. It was a cross between a juke joint and a gentleman's lounge. The vibe inside was cozy and sexy and laidback and maybe a little bit seedy but it was a good kind of seedy. All Maurice wanted was a drink but sometimes what you want and what you get is not the same thing.

He had been having this feeling lately that he just could not shake. He had found one of Max's business cards under a couch cushion. He knew he didn't leave it there. *"Why would Amanda need a lawyer? She wants a divorce,"* he kept thinking to himself. Things have been difficult but apart from the no sex thing they were doing well. He had to stop having sex with Amanda because he contracted herpes from some girl he hooked up with in Vegas. He had never given her a reason other than he was not in the mood.

He sat at the bar and had a couple of drinks racking his brain without saying much more than exactly what he wanted from the bartender. The bartender tried to make small talk with him a few times but her attempts were futile. She was persistent though.

"I hope you know it's kinda rude that this whole time I been here just trying to do my job and you just been ignoring me." Her southern twang came out.

Maurice glanced up at her. She was almost as old as his mother. Maybe not as old but she had that same old school vibe about her. Maurice felt trapped in his life, he did not want to get a divorce because of the impact it may have on Alliyah. Maybe she could drop a few jewels on him, that's what bartenders do right? He squinted, trying his best to guess her age. He guessed she was approaching fifty; mid-forties at best.

"What? You're trying to guess my age right?"

"No, not at all, why would I want to do that?" Maurice liked her attitude. He smiled.

"See, see how much things can change when you just relax." She chucked him on the shoulder from across the bar. "Stop being so mad at the world?" she smiled; she had a beautiful set of pearly whites with a gold cap on her second incisor.

"Mad at the world." Maurice loosened his tie. "I'm not mad at the world, just thinking about some things that's all."

"What you thinking about pumpkin?" She really wanted to know. "You look like you got it all together; nice suit, nice watch, looking like you work on Wall Street, what you really got to worry about?"

Maurice smiled again, she seemed so carefree.

"What's your name sweetie?" She flirted with Maurice.

Maurice paused. *"Is this old ass woman flirting with me?"*

The truth is she was not that old. She was just very country, which kind of translates into old. Not old-old just country-old.

"Maurice Porter," he said while looking her in the eye.

"Maybeline," she replied and sashayed down the full length of the bar to get a wet rag. Maurice being the man that he was watched her ass all the way there.

"So what's on ya mind?" Maybeline said cleaning up and getting ready to leave for the evening. Her replacement had just walked in.

Maurice looked down the bar and saw Maybeline's replacement coming towards them.

"Seems like you gotta go."

"That's fine we can talk." Maybeline poured herself a drink and headed towards the back of the venue.

She signaled Maurice to follow. He did. Sitting down in the corner of the candle lit room Maybeline was a different person than she was behind the bar. She seemed younger. Maurice sat across from her. They were tucked into a very intimate corner. Old sixties hits curled around the dim lights in the room. Maybeline was having cognac straight. Maurice was having vodka and cranberry. Maurice told Maybeline about his marriage or what was left of his marriage, told her that he had not had sex with his wife for more than a year. Maybeline shook her head in disappointment.

"Well, let me tell you something, if you have a wife and you ain't fucked her in a year, someone out there will, believe me honey." Maybeline was on her second cognac by that time and she was getting very honest.

"It's not that I don't want to, I can't."

"What do you mean you can't, like your dick don't work?" Maybeline pulled back to get a good look at Maurice.

"No no, my dick works fine." Maurice gestured to assure her his dick worked; he could not tell her the truth in that moment.

"Hmm does it?" She smiled a cognac smile, and watched Maurice with new eyes.

Maurice saw it in her body language but he pretended he did not see it, *"Is she trying to fuck me?"* he thought to himself. She was not his type but something about her was appealing. Her bravery, her gall, her sass whatever it is called was turning him on. And she knew it. She was working her magic. She sat back and watched him.

The tables around them vanished. The darkness tightened around them. Feet approached, a floating hand placed two new drinks in front of both of them. They sat and stared each other down in silence. Maurice could feel Maybeline's sexual energy creeping into his blood. He sipped his drink and as the flavor relaxed into his taste buds he could taste her and smell her. She saw the look on his face. And *Bang.*

"Let's go somewhere where we can really talk." Her eyes said it all.

"What do you have in mind?" Maurice was trying his best to delay.

"My place, I live like two blocks from here." She knew she had him at *"my place"*.

This young boy had no chance against her game. She had decided the moment he walked in that she was taking him home but she was not going to make him any wiser. She took up her purse and he followed her round ass.

She lived in a dingy apartment two blocks away, a second floor walkup. Maurice had not seen a place this dingy ever. She shared her apartment with her son who was twenty two. Maurice was approaching thirty two. Her son was on the couch in the living room playing Play Station. When Maybeline walked in; he sucked his teeth and pretended not to see that she was not alone.

Maurice said, "Hey!" and in the back of his mind he felt like shit.

Here he was on his way to fuck this guy's mom and the nerve of him to say hello.

"Sup," he gave him the chin up.

"You going out tonight?" Maybeline was sending a signal. "That's my son Trey."

Maurice was barely ten years older than Trey. And for some reason this fact turned Maurice on. Trey clicked the game off and moved toward the door. As soon as the door closed behind him, Maurice and Maybeline attacked each other. She threw him onto the couch and mounted him, he flipped her over and when their lips locked she injected him with her beautiful serum, the sweet harmony of cognac and tongue.

He momentarily lost his mind. She spread her legs and welcomed him in. He slipped her panties to the side and plunged into her slowly.

She moaned. "You dirty mother fucker, give me that sweet young dick."

Maurice could not believe he was inside this old ass woman with no condom. I hope she can't get pregnant. He kept thinking. But her pussy was doing things to his mind that put that thought on hold.

Maurice looked up and saw all the dinge and chaos of the room and in some twisted way the experience felt primal. She was showing him a side of himself he had not seen in a long time. He took a deep breath and went in with all his might.

Chapter Twenty Nine

Max walked into Cornerstone. He knew Brenton would be upstairs. He met Marla and KEV on the stairs.

"Hey how are you…" He didn't remember her name.

"Yow KEV what's up?" It was a little awkward on the narrow stairs.

"I'm good, you know, chillin. Brenton is by the bar." KEV wanted Max to know he had to leave.

Max got the message. "So, I'll see ya'll around, I guess." They were gone before Max could finish.

"Yeah."

Max watched them descend the stairs. Brenton was talking to the bald Mexican bartender with the Taliban beard.

"So you manage KEV?" The bartender sounded excited.

"Nah, I just book him, but every now and then I do a few things that could be like management but I'm not his manager."

"That's fuckin' cool bro, next drink is on me; by the way I'm Jose. Nice to meet you man, what were they doing an article on him." Jose's eyes lit up.

"Yeah, he is about to totally blow right now, when the white people start listening, I mean listening hard, that's when the real money comes."

Brenton was still thinking about Emily. He looked at his phone, scrolled through and found her number. Should he call her? He was not sure, but he wanted to, he did not want to seem desperate. He never called women anyway, what was he thinking. Then he was like fuck it, and just as he was about to hit call. Max came strolling in. Brenton exhaled, took a sip from his drink then greeted Max.

Max sat down. He was still reeling from the flood of energy in his body from the threesome but his brain was still in crash landing mode, with regard to Amanda. He looked a little confused.

"What you drinking?" Max slapped down his credit card on the bar. "Leave it open." He gave Jose a chin up.

"Hennessy, KEV got me drinking this shit." Brenton looked at his glass with reluctance.

"I do not fuck with dark liquor, ever," Max said.

"Me neither, but this Hennessey is not bad."

"Well the last time I had dark liquor, let's just say the night ended in prayers, serious prayers."

"Prayers?" Brenton gave Max that, *how bad could it have been* look.

"Man, I was at this loft party in Dumbo, I am not sure if the party was sponsored by the liquor company or if it was just a theme party and the liquor was featured but all they had was dark liquor. It was pretty smooth going down but when I got home that whole shit just hit."

Jose and Brenton started laughing.

"This shit was not funny. When I got home and went to sleep; my bed would not stop spinning, shit was like the exorcist!"

"I know man, I have had a few nights like that, Long Island Ice Teas do that to me," Jose said in a sympathetic voice.

"But that was not the crazy part. The crazy part was when that dark liquor kicked into third gear. My bed stopped spinning and started sliding across the floor then slid up against the wall then went onto the ceiling."

Brenton and Jose were dying with laughter. "No fucking way," Brenton covered his mouth while he laughed.

"So now I am on my bed on my ceiling holding on to the bed trying not to fall from the ceiling to the floor." Max did not have an ounce of laugher in his tone but in the back of his mind you could tell he was laughing at the experience. "That's why I am having a Stella; you cannot get that drunk on just beer unless you have like twenty."

Brenton and Jose shook their heads in agreement. Jose handed Max a Stella.

Max's phone buzzed. It was a text from Amanda, *"Today was amazing, let's meet for lunch again tomorrow same place same time, we don't even have to talk."* A cold chill came over Max. He was slowly realizing how serious this Amanda situation was.

"So what's up man?" Brenton patted Max on the shoulder.

"Not much," Max replied.

He was trying to think of what to write back to Amanda. *"I am not going to meet you Amanda, please do not text or call my phone again."*

"What do you mean, not much, you said you wanted to talk right?"

"Yeah, it's crazy bro." Max narrowed his eyes.

"Come on, bring it." Brenton had that, *I can handle it* look on his face. His phone rang. Brenton ignored the ring.

"I don't even know where to start." Max took another sip from his Stella.

"Start from the end?" Brenton said with a chuckle.

"This is serious man." Max looked at Brenton.

Jose was busying himself with two other customers down the bar but he was listening to their conversation.

"I am serious, start from where you are now, that way you get the surprise or the shock out of the way." Brenton went into business mode.

This was why Max was here, he knew Brenton did not like to bullshit and beat around the bush.

"Ok here goes." Max took another sip. "Amanda is blackmailing me."

"Amanda?" Brenton rolled the idea around in his head. "Blackmailing? That's some spy novel shit right there. Amanda? Why would Amanda want to…? Oh damn." It all came crashing into Brenton's head.

Max was shaking his head in disappointment.

"You fucked Amanda?"

Brenton spoke a little louder than he expected. The other two people at the bar looked over. Jose looked over also.

"Another drink?" he asked.

Brenton said, "Yes."

"What? How did that happen?" Brenton was befuddled. "I'm guessing Maurice doesn't know right?"

"No he doesn't" Max said with reluctance.

"So what happened?"

"It's a long story man," Max said in a lazy voice.

Brenton looked at Max then looked at his drink then looked at his missed call. It was Emily. He wanted to call her back but he knew his boy needed him.

"Damn, where do I start? Damn." Max took a deep breath then exhaled. "So like a month ago, I was supposed to meet Maurice at his place. It was about six, seven around there, no it was seven. So I get there and Amanda is there and you know how Amanda be looking."

Brenton agreed but with a little bit of reticence.

"So she offers me a drink and we start talking. I have known Amanda for years, I mean since her freshman year at Syracuse. We had always flirted but kinda just as a joke, nothing serious. But for some reason that day I don't know what happened. I said something about a drink and she responded that she needed a drink also or something like that."

Brenton kinda knew where this was going.

"And the whole time I am thinking it was a joke and them she just threw it on me!"

"What do you mean she threw it on you?" Brenton knew there was more to the story.

"Basically she was like, *fuck me*, but not in those words." Max had an honest look on his face.

"You coulda said no Max, you coulda said no," Brenton said in his best disapproving voice.

"I know, I tried, but she was so…"

Max closed his eyes and even though Amanda was trying to blackmail him he could not resist the thought of wanting her. He loved the fact that she was so upfront about what she wanted.

"She came at me so hard man, and I know its Maurice's wife but the shit happened so fast and by the time I realized what was happening it was too late."

"So this happened a month ago right?" Brenton felt like there was more.

"Yeah, but." Max knew that this next part was what Brenton was going judge him for.

Brenton saw it coming. "And you been fucking her ever since, and now you want to stop and she is like nope, no fucking way, and she's like let's continue, and you are like Maurice is my boy, and she is like you should have thought about that before you fucked me, and you are like but now I realize what I have done wrong and I wanna stop now, and she is like fuck that if we stop I tell everybody. And the truth is you don't really give a fuck about losing your friendship with Maurice you're just worried about losing Sophie, that about get it right?" Brenton said all that in about five seconds flat then took a sip of his rum and coke.

Max agreed. He smiled a sad smile.

Brenton had one last pressing question. "By the way how was the pussy?"

"Ah, man. It was fucking amazing," Max said as he shrugged.

Chapter Thirty

"Yeah, I am at Cornerstone."

"Cornerstone? I have never been in there."

"You have never been to Cornerstone?"

"I use to, way back in the days when it was Brooklyn Mod."

"Wow, you been around here that long?"

"Yeah, my family's been around here before it got gentrified."

"So this whole place is completely different than it was back then right?"

"Totally different, but it's not too bad now."

"Hmmm, where are you?"

"Home."

"And how is the boyfriend?"

"He is not here he went to LA for a meeting."

"Meeting, what does he do?"

"He's a comedian."

"Funny?"

"He is."

"I guess he has to be right?"

"That's his job. Matter of fact, I just spoke with him, told him I was gonna hang out with you?"

Brenton's heart jumped. "And what did he say?"

"He said enjoy."

And *Bang*. Brenton was teleported into Emily's Apartment.

Chapter Thirty One

"Hey, Max," Maurice said into his phone.

"What's up Maurice?"

Max was standing outside of Cornerstone. He was checking his text messages when his phone rang.

Maurice was walking back from Maybelline's crummy apartment. He felt dirty just thinking about it. The humidity made him feel even grosser. Why did he fuck her? Why did he fuck her without a condom? He knew why, but he could not admit it. Knowing a thing and admitting it are two different things.

"I need to talk to you man."

"What, what's up?" Max was suspicious about what Maurice wanted to talk about. *"Maybe he knows,"* Max thought to himself.

Maurice did not want to tell Max about the card. He wanted to see if Max was going to tell him what was going on.

"Nothing, just wanna talk, just some crazy shit happening."

Maurice felt that Max had betrayed him. Max was supposed to be his mentor, his boy. How could he have kept something like this from him.

There was a brief silence, Max was thinking about what to say next.

"You wanna meet now?" He was hoping Maurice would say no.

A text landed on his phone, *"Tomorrow at the diner, ok baby."* It was Amanda.

"Fuck it, why not. Where are you?" Maurice asked.

"I'm on Dekalb."

"Can you meet me at that place down the block from Brenton's in like an hour?" Maurice tried to sound as friendly as he could.

"What spot?" Max controlled the trembling in his voice.

"The Emerson."

"The Emerson, The Emerson, yeah, yeah cool, cool."

Max's mind slipped back to the day Amanda asked him to meet her there. She showed up in an extremely short slinky dress. She told him to wait for her in the back. It was pretty early in the evening. There were only two patrons and the bartender there. The Emerson had that old Irish pub feel. She walked in quietly. Went directly to the bar and ordered two shots of vodka. Max sat in the back in the raised platform area and watched her.

"So what do you want to do?" Amanda asked as if it was a multiple choice question.

"Have a seat." He gently touched the spot next to him as he looked up at her perfectly curvaceous body.

"I can't sit." Amanda smiled and shifted her weight onto her right leg.

"Why?" Max slid his hand between her thighs.

Amanda shifted her weight onto her left leg as his hand got closer and closer to her vagina. She was dripping wet. He was about to find out.

"Continue," she said slowly.

And *Bang*. Max's index finger brushed the soft mouth of her freshly shaven pussy and it was pure liquid silk. He closed his eyes, took a deep breath and savored the feeling.

"I have to go to the bathroom, I think you should definitely, definitely come help me figure out what we should do."

She walked slowly toward the bathroom.

Chapter Thirty Two

Max's phone rang. It was Amanda. Max was in the lobby of his building.

"What the fuck is going on with this girl?" Max was upset.

He was not going to answer. He got on the elevator. His phone rang the entire time. Max and Sophie lived on the twelfth floor of the newest building in Clinton Hill, *163 Washington Avenue.* As he exited the elevator his phone started ringing again.

"Yes!"

"So we are on for lunch tomorrow right?"

"Like I said, I am done, finished, can you please stop fuckin' calling me?"

"Ok babe, see you tomorrow."

Amanda hung up her phone and turned to Sophie. "Sorry had to make sure my lunch plans were confirmed with Maurice."

"Oh, Maurice, how is everything with him? I see the stock market is doing well."

They both laughed.

Max opened the door and his body was instantly covered in a cold sweat. He had to hurry and gather his nerves. He stood by the door for a few seconds, then turned and headed toward Amanda and Sophie who were sitting on the couch in the living room having wine.

"Hey Amanda, how are you?"

They exchanged kisses.

"I am good. It's been a while, how are you?" Amanda spoke as if she had not seen him in months. "Wow are you putting on some weight."

She touched his stomach. Normally Sophie would have taken that as Amanda flirting but she no longer saw Amanda as a threat.

"Weight? No."

"I kid," Amanda shot back.

"Baby how was your day?" Sophie gave Max a big hug.

"Long day babe, long day," Max said while watching Amanda over Sophie's shoulder.

The whole time he gave her the evil eye.

"Sophie, tell Max what we were talking about." Amanda touched Sophie on the thigh gently. Max saw her hand and narrowed his eyes. Amanda bit into her lip

"Oh yeah, so you know how I have been trying to get people to come in and speak to the girls."

"Yes?" Max was fuming on the inside. *Who the fuck does Amanda think she is?"*

"I totally forgot that Amanda had been a teen mom, but after we spoke today we are putting together a kind of mentorship program in which she can come in on weekends and speak with the girls, maybe mentor a few of them, something like that."

Max looked at Amanda. In his mind he was calling her every name in the book but outwardly he congratulated her and smiled.

"Amanda, can I speak to Sophie for a second?" Max took Sophie by the arm and they went off into the bedroom.

"I thought you did not like Amanda?" Max whispered.

"That was when I thought you were fucking her, but now I realize that that was just me being insecure. Amanda is totally harmless, she is such a sweetie," Sophie said in earnest.

Max did not know what to do. "It's your call but I just think…" Max realized how ridiculous he was beginning to sound.

"Babe," Sophie put both hands around Max's waist and looked up at him, "you gotta trust me."

"But."

Max decided to stop. His phone buzzed in his pocket. Sophie pressed the bedroom door closed. She slowly unzipped Max's pants.

"Amanda is in the living room."

Max took his phone out of his pocket.

Sophie took his dick into her mouth. Max closed his eyes as she licked up and down and jerked him gently trying not to make too much noise. Sophie was sure Amanda could hear the slurping through the door. That was her intention.

Max placed one hand on Sophie's head as he gently thrust into her mouth. Sophie gagged a little. Amanda definitely heard that.

Max looked at his phone. *"Lunch tomorrow?"*

Amanda was sure this time Max would have to say yes.

"Yes." Max partially lost his erection.

Sophie looked up at him. "What?"

"Amanda is outside," he mouthed to her.

"Ok, ok, let me stop." Sophie stood up.

She could feel her inner freak twirling around inside her body, her nipples were on fire; her pussy was jumping. It was almost as if she was being possessed.

Sophie and Max walked back into the living room. Amanda was on the couch smiling at her glass of wine.

"Well listen I have to go meet..." Max decided to edit himself, "someone at The Emerson"

"The Emerson, where is that?" Amanda asked, filled with curiosity.

"It's no too far from here," Max replied.

"Ok, babe." Sophie kissed Max on the lips and he was out the door.

Amanda unbuttoned the top button of her blouse. Sophie sat next to her and took up her glass of wine.

Chapter Thirty Three

"We need to talk."

"I know."

"Can I come over?"

"No it is probably best if we met somewhere in public."

Meghan was hoping she could see Sophie alone.

"Meet me at Peaches."

"When?"

"In twenty minutes."

Peaches is in Bed-Stuy. It is a modern soul food fusion restaurant. Meghan was early. She sat by the bar. The bartender entertained her until Sophie arrived. Meghan kept her eye on the street. Peaches was spacious and had huge windows. The décor was some form of modern antique. When Sophie got out the cab on Lewis Avenue Meghan lit up. She could not hold it in any more. She was just going to let Sophie know exactly how she felt. In her mind it went something like:

"Sophie I have been in love with you since the first day I met you." And Sophie would say, *"Meghan I have felt the same way about you."*

After that it would be all bliss and hours and hours of passionate love making.

But that was in her head.

Sophie spotted Meghan and hurried over to her. They hugged like old friends, like ex-lovers seeing each other again after a long time. It had only been a few hours since they were feasting on each other in a threesome with Max.

The restaurant was crowded. They were at the bar for a few minutes before they got a table. They had already had some wine before they sat down.

Max walked into The Emerson. Maurice was already there. He was sitting in the back in the raised platform area. The irony almost saddened Max. Deep in his heart he wanted to come clean. He wanted to tell Maurice exactly what happened and let the chips fall where they may. How could he do it? How do you tell your best friend that you are fucking his wife?

Max sat down in front of Maurice. Maurice did not say a word for a while.

"You good?"

Max tried to break the uneasiness. "Nah."

Maurice was trying to make Max as uneasy as he could. This was the only way he was going to get him to come clean about Amanda seeking Max's advice about divorce.

"So, what's going on man?" Maurice grinded his

teeth.

Max could see the grimace on his face.

"What do you mean?"

Max sat back and looked him dead in the eye. If Maurice wanted to know anything he was going to have to ask.

"You know what I mean."

Maurice sat back also.

"Nope, I have no idea."

Max folded his arms across his chest.

"So you are telling me that you know nothing about..." Maurice placed the business card on the table and looked Max dead in the eyes.

Max realized that it was his card. He started shaking a little on the inside.

"What does that have to do with anything?" Max said incredulously.

"The least you could do is be straight with me Max."

Maurice raised his voice and slammed is palms against the table as he stood. Max swallowed slowly and gritted his teeth.

"Listen man," Max was searching for the right words.

"The least you could have done is warned me man, I know you have attorney client confidentially and all that bullshit but dude I am your boy, we're like family."

"I, I..." Max was stunned when he realized that Maurice was not confronting him about Amanda.

"All this time we been friends man and you are plotting behind my back to have my wife divorce me."

"Listen, Maurice, I swear I am not plotting to get you divorced. She just asked me about a few things and I told her to call me and maybe I could put her in touch with someone who could help."

Max was still trembling on the inside. His mouth was dry.

"And you couldn't tell me, huh?" Maurice had a look of disappointment on his face. "All I'm saying is if the roles were reversed I would have given you a heads up, ok."

Maurice stood up again. Max closed his eyes and took a deep breath.

Meghan looked around the room at the diners. Everyone was in their own little world. She marveled at how beautiful everyone was, but these people were nothing compared to this woman in front of her.

"So where do we start?" Sophie was direct.

The timid unsure Sophie was nowhere to be found in her person. Meghan was intimidated by Sophie's confidence.

The evening outside was begging to come inside. The humid night, the beautiful people, the wait staff moving about with such precision, glasses clinking, the laughter, the music pouring out of the speakers, the loud patrons at the bar, it all screamed Brooklyn.

Sophie surveyed the room. She felt like a predator. The men were beautiful. The women looked tasty. No one was safe under her gaze. She realized that she loved Max but the world she occupied now had become so much bigger.

Meghan was sweating; tiny beads of sweat were beginning to form on her nose. Sophie saw it and smiled. Sophie's brain was whizzing at a million miles per second.

"I think we should talk about what happened today."

"Ok go ahead, what happened today?" Sophie was ice cold. She could sense how needy Meghan had become.

Meghan reached across the table and touched Sophie's hand. Stevie Wonder came on over the speaker. *Ribbon In The Sky*. It seemed as if this moment was tailored for them. Meghan smiled. Sophie smiled back at her.

"I am not sure how to say this Sophie, I think I have been getting more and more attached to you and after today I am not sure what I think. The truth is I really, really love you Sophie and in a million years I never thought I would have been able to say this to anyone but I truly love you and I am not asking you to do anything about it, I just wanted you to know." Meghan ended as the song ended.

Sophie patted Meghan's hand. She thought about all those years they had been friends. She loved Meghan but not like that. They were friends and casual lovers, but she knew what Meghan wanted and she knew she could not give it to her.

"Meghan, what do you expect me to do with what you just said?"

"Nothing, I just want you to know."

"No, that's not it, I think you want me to leave Max."

Sophie was in full control of her thoughts. "I think you want me and you to get together?"

"And what is wrong with wanting that Sophie?"

"Nothing is wrong with it. It is just that it's unrealistic."

Sophie took a sip of her wine.

Meghan's chest tightened inside. "Why is it unrealistic Sophie?"

Sophie closed her eyes and thought for a second. "Meghan if we got together how long it would last?"

"I am not sure, but it is worth a try right?" Meghan had a pitiful tone in her voice. And *Bang*

Sophie was back in the bathroom at Outpost. She was remembering the first time she kissed Meghan. An electric current ran through her body. She wanted to savor that memory because the Meghan she knew was no longer in the restaurant with her. Meghan had lost her confidence and it made her seem weak and nothing is sexy about being weak.

"Don't waste your time Meghan; I would never leave my man for you. I am not saying we can't be friends but leave my man, no way."

Meghan felt the dagger plunge deep into her heart. Her eyes filled with water.

"I think I am going to leave now, ok."

Sophie grabbed her hand. "Meghan, think about what you are asking me to do? What is wrong with what we have right now?"

Meghan emptied her glass of wine and walked out. She expected Sophie to follow her. Sophie didn't.

Chapter Thirty Four

Emily answered her door in a white t-shirt. Brenton could not control himself. Emily lived on the first floor of an old brownstone. From the outside, the brownstone looked like any other brownstone on the block. But once you entered it was a whole different world.

The floors were white through and through. The furnishings were sparse but beautiful. It was as if she went traveling the world and handpicked every piece. The entire floor was one huge open space. There were windows at the front and at the back and bare brick walls on both sides. She had designer couches and post-modern looking chairs one would likely see in movies about the future. Emily was the prototype of the modern woman.

"Wow, what is it you said you did again?"

She smiled. "I am an international spy."

Brenton played along. "And what mission are you on at the moment?"

"Mission? I think the mission can be whatever you want." She walked toward him and pressed her breast against his chest. "As long as it is not missionary," she whispered into his ear.

She did something to him. Something no other woman had ever done. She was clever, sophisticated, yes, but something about her sexual energy made him clay in her hands. Emily knew exactly how she impacted men, and sometimes women. They would love who she was but then they would try to contain her. She hated containment. That's why she chose the career she chose. She was a personal trainer. She specifically trained stars. She loved travel and the finer things in life.

Brenton spun her around and pressed her against the front door.

"So agent Dangerfield, what would you do if I told you; you are over dressed for this mission."

Brenton held her hands above her head and pressed his pelvis against her. She felt his bulging erection.

"I would say you are lying." She looked up at him smiling.

He narrowed his eyes.

"I came dressed in exactly what I need to get this mission done." She moaned a little.

He spun her around again. This time she was facing the door, her hands still held above her head. He was behind her. She pressed her ass against his erection. Brenton chuckled. He knew she was in for some serious trouble.

He used his foot to gently kick her legs open, she willingly obliged, she even pressed her ass back some more. Her ass was barely covered by the t-shirt when she leaned over. From his vantage point he could see that she had no underwear on.

He got on his knees behind her and bit into her ass muscle. She gyrated and moaned as his teeth sank into her. He passed his nose gently across her ass cheeks a few time then bit into the other cheek, she moaned even harder.

By this time she was bent all the way over with her hands still pressed against the door. He passed the stubble on his face against her inner thigh and moved it up and down, up and down, up and down slowly and gently. She was falling into a trance. He could hear her insides begging for him to enter her. Brenton was in no hurry, he was planning on truly enjoying this evening with Emily.

He licked the flesh of her inner thighs then nibbled on the area just a few micro meters away from her labia. She was writhing and moaning and gyrating. He passed his thumb gently through her dripping wet pussy, he spread her wide open. And *Bang*.

It was a half hour later and she was on her back trembling, Brenton had kissed and licked every inch of her body. She already had four orgasms and he had not even entered her as yet. Emily was looking up at the roof in tears. She had finally met her match. She had finally met someone who knew her body; he touched her perfectly. In her mind she kind of knew that he might have been amazing in bed but this, this was too much.

Brenton heard her sobbing. In his heart he smiled, sat up next to her and gently rubbed her stomach.

"Why are you crying agent Dangerfield?"

"Stop!" She chucked him and smiled.

He climbed on top of her and pressed her hands against the bed. They froze for a moment and it felt like they had known each other for eons.

He kissed her gently. And *Bang*.

Chapter Thirty Five

It was high noon. Brooklyn. Downtown. Not too
far from the Barclay's Center. The sidewalks are
all warped from the heat. The asphalt is soft and
bubbly. The A/C inside the diner at the corner of
third and Atlantic is blowing at full blast. The old
radio is piping out something from the fifties. The
Spanish cooks in the back are dancing to a different
tune. The entire diner smells like pancakes and
nostalgia. The old waitress is dragging her old
bones to a table with two construction workers.

Amanda's bag and purse are sitting across from
an empty seat that was once indented by the weight
of a six foot two inches tall; well-manicured black
male. His name is Max. Yes Max.

Max and Amanda are in a familiarly awkward
position in the basement of the diner. They are in
the bathroom. Amanda is bent over with her nails
clamped onto the ceramic basin. Max is grunting
and she's moaning quietly toward some primal,
pyric orgasm. He is going at her with a vengeance.

This is a brutal and sadistic exchange. Clinical.
Emotionless. But below all the mechanics of this

beautiful maneuver is the subtext of a man fucking the living daylights out of his best friend's wife, simply because she is *forcing* him to do so.

The people on the floor above could feel the tension moving up through the floor boards. It was almost as if the tremors sliding off the tip of his dick as he entered her could peel the tiles off the walls.

The construction workers bit into the sandwiches with sexual ease. The sweaty Spanish cooks moved to the music in the kitchen with such sexual fervor it was as if they were aroused by the sound of the strips of bacon frying.

Max had a hand full of Amanda's hair. Amanda could feel her insides tightening around his dick. She grunted and Max plunged into her harder and harder. And *Bang*.

They both froze as their respective orgasms rendered their muscles useless. Max grabbed her breasts from behind and arched his back as he released inside of her. He sighed. She gyrated slowly against him. He pulled out and looked down on his dick with shame. Dragged the condom off his dick and threw it into the toilet. He looked at Amanda through the mirror. He hated her. But that pussy was so good. He fucking hated her. She smiled and looked at him with giddy eyes as she fixed her hair.

"I need to figure this shit out," Max said to himself.

Chapter Thirty Six

"So what's your plan?" Brenton asked.

Max had a dazed look on his face. "Man, I have no idea."

It was Tuesday evening; they were sitting at the bar in the Brooklyn Moon. The heat was serious about it being the end of August. The doors were flung wide-open. The makeshift sidewalk garden that hugged the entrance of the Brooklyn Moon was not big or strong enough to hold the heat outside. The trendy after work crowd was traipsing in slowly.

A group of single black women; a pair of single white girls on the pull; the pretentious artsy type trying too hard at being cool; the politicos by the bar talking too loud, spewing their leftist agenda from their well ironed bow tied necks; this was vintage Brooklyn Moon.

The air was filled with rancor and delight. The entire room smelled like a surrealist kitchen. The servers walked past Brenton and Max with mountains on plates, mountains that made their mouths water. Streaming into the room from a pair of invisible speakers were some sweet reggae vibes.

"So what happened today man?"

"She was like come and meet her so I went, I can't believe this is happening to me man, for real." Max's voice drifted off.

"Nigga you know you wanted to go." Brenton was trying to cheer him up. "But fo' real though, that's kinda foul man."

Max thought about it for a while. "I know, I know."

"You should tell Maurice, get that shit over with." Brenton shrugged and looked at Max.

"It ain't Maurice I am worried about."

Max thought about Sophie standing in their living room with one leg cocked up on the arm of the sofa in her crotch-less get up.

"Sophie, Sophie would definitely leave me." He looked up from his Stella. "I can't lose her now."

"This is gonna be a crazy juggle then man."

"I know, you gotta help me bro." Max seemed to be pleading.

"Well I can tell you this much, she would not be pressing you this hard if you was not fucking her so good. That's how a lot of you mothafuckas get fucked up in the game." Brenton was like a sage in this moment.

"What do you mean?" Max was taken aback.

"Not every girl should get, or even deserves the A dick," Brenton said it like it was wisdom straight from God.

"What? What do you mean by the A dick?" Max was curious.

"Listen man, if you not trying to lock her down, never give her the A dick. You gotta give her the C dick at best, but never the A dick. Matter of fact you should not even give her the B dick." Sage Brenton was in perfect form.

"Where do you get this dick grading system from?" Max was lost.

"Every man knows how he feels about a woman right?" Brenton was very matter of fact.

"Yes." Max was in agreement.

"Well, you gotta fuck em according to how you feel. Case and point, you can't fuck your best friend's wife like you are trying to marry her; that would be wrong. You gotta fuck her like you was just trying to get a nut, that way she know where shit stands, not that I would ever fuck my best friend's wife." Brenton was laughing a little as he said this.

"I am fucking serious man." Max was begging for a little bit of gravitas.

"I am fucking serious too bro. You gotta pick and choose who you give the A dick, or you will be in constant problems. These women out here are trying to get laid right. They not much different than we, they just trying to get a little dick and go on about their way, but when you start putting down dick like you trying to marry them they will act accordingly." Brenton hit the nail on the head.

"Oh shit." Max got exactly what he was saying. "So in other words you are saying I need to underperform?"

"Exactly." Brenton was proud of himself.

"So, in order to get Amanda off my dick, so to speak, I need to..."

"Yes, you need to give her that D dick." Brenton cut in before Max could finish his sentence.

Max had a quick flash back of his get-together with Amanda at the diner.

Chapter Thirty Seven

"Yow. KEV listen, I am throwing this party next week brah. It's kind of a celebration for your trip, plus my cousin Trace is visiting from the UK. It's gonna be the party of the year man. I need you to come through and bring some nice ladies." Brenton said all that in about zero seconds.

He was mostly excited though because his cousin Trace was going to be visiting. KEV had been smoking weed all morning so getting excited was not on his list of priorities.

"Bet, I'll come through and I'll bring some bad bitches."

"KEV, you the fucking man, brah." Brenton was grateful.

Having KEV at the party would definitely add a certain amount of baller-ness to his party, not that it needed it.

KEV hung up and looked at the young lady on his couch fixing her hair.

"So, you saying you gon' get me those new J's right?" She tried to look as sexy as she could.

KEV's eyes were barely open. "Anything you want mah, anything you want."

She smiled, narrowed her eyes and tilted her head. He looked at her reassuringly.

"I got you, don't worry."

She said, "Ok, you promise right."

She reached into his zipper. And *Bang*. He was totally flaccid. She closed her eyes, took a deep breath and…

"Yow. Check this out. Party next week, my roof. 9pm. It's BYOB. You have to have at least two girls with you to get in also."

"Brenton this is me, I gotta have two girls?" Max felt a little disrespected.

"No, no, not you, I am just saying for dudes who are coming. You family man. You don't gotta do shit." Brenton was apologetic.

They both laughed.

"I'll bring Sophie, maybe her girl Meghan will roll with us." Max thought about the threesome with Sophie and Meghan.

"Tell a few people cause this one is gonna be the craziest party ever." Brenton was absolutely sure.

The Craziest Party EVER
139 Emerson
The Penthouse
Sat Aug 25th, 9pm
BYOB

*Dudes can only enter
accompanied by two women.

It is amazing how much trouble can start based on a simple text. Brenton hit send, as his text riffled through the nonchalant streets of Brooklyn, then he smiled.

Chapter Thirty Eight

In Brooklyn there is a church on every corner. Every bible thumping scoundrel thinks they are the next John the Baptist. At all hours of the day and night these fledgling ministers, compelled by the spirit of the "Lord" will burst into fits of preaching on the train like some sleeper cell of Jesus distributors.

It just so happens that tonight was one of those nights when one of said diviners would cross paths with a broken and vulnerable Meghan.

Meghan has never believed much in the way of religion except for that one time in college, but when you are at your weakest; belief is sometimes all you have. Her heart was a soft and weeping lump of flesh, when like an angel sent from MTA heaven, Pastor Cox was hit by the spirit.

He sprung to his feet like a mind controlled special operations assassin in an Episcopal sleep walk.

"Ladies and gentleman," Pastor Cox was hesitant, "I am Pastor Emanuel Cox. I have never done this before but I think someone on this train needs to hear this message. It is stated in scripture the twenty third psalm: the Lord is my shepherd, I shall not want."

He scanned the train car. The passengers were trying their best to not make eye contact. Normally Meghan would not have given this guy a second of her day but for some reason everything he said was related to her. He was there for her.

He repeated himself. "The Lord is my shepherd I shall not want, and that want is a promise. It did not say I shall maybe, or I shall sometimes, no, it says..." He went into full preacher mode.

Meghan wondered what force was behind his convictions. What was pushing this man? This young man, he could not have been older than thirty five, to commit this act of self-sacrifice in this public space.

"...not. I shall NOT want. He lay me down beside the still waters, he restoreth my soul. Restoreth my soul. To restore means to fix, to make new, to bring something back to its original condition."

He paused for effect. There was no effect.

By this time Pastor Emanuel Cox was having a one on one conversation with Meghan. He had lost the entire train car. People were busying themselves scrolling through pictures on their phones, reading upside down newspapers, reading ads; they were busy doing everything but listening.

"Why would the lord have to restore something or someone?" He looked around the train car. "The lord knows that every now and then through no fault of our own we get broken."

Meghan knew for certain that he was there specifically for her.

"Nigga shut the fuck up man," some young guy shouted from the other end of the car. "It's almost fucking twelve man, I gotta hear this shit twenty four seven, come on man."

The train car chuckled. Meghan felt sorry for Pastor Cox. He quietly reached into his bag and started handing out small flyers to whoever he thought would take them. Meghan took a flyer. And *Bang*. She knew it. This man was going to change her life.

The moment they touched she was back in Atlanta. He had that same energy that Rev. Nathaniel Tatum had. Rev. Tatum was a one of a kind person. He was a minister but in another incarnation he could have been a pimp. His words were always direct. He said what he meant and he meant what he said, every single time. He was born and bred in Biloxi Mississippi. He was as slick as a fraternity of oil rigs. He got kicked out of the military when he was twenty nine years old, became a minister, built a church from scratch, made a fortune, then lost it to a scandal. Sex scandal.

Meghan was in the office of Rev. Tatum doing paper work. The office was stuck in the basement all the way in the back of the Church. The Reverend was not in, so Meghan had kicked off her shoes and was taking it easy. It was an average fall evening in Atlanta.

When the Reverend got in and saw how relaxed Meghan was in his office, something inside his head, and inside his pants, moved. Yes, Reverend Tatum was married and yes Meghan was only twenty, but the Reverend had his ways and his ways were his ways. So when he walked in and she was perched on a stool trying to replace books on a top shelf, the Reverend had no choice but to approach her from behind and clasp her around the waist. Meghan was frightened to no end, but something about this old man's hands pressed gently against her pelvis felt so sexual and wrong that it turned her on.

She heard the Reverend breathing against her neck. She could hear the Reverend's wife and the other women who worked at the church milling about in the other rooms.

"I will split your shit wide open," The Reverend whispered into her ear. And *Bang*.

Before Meghan knew it, this old man had her spread eagle on his desk and was preaching a slow sermon in her clit.

"Next stop is Franklin Ave." The mechanical voice over the speaker reminded everyone.

Meghan was jolted back into the subway car. Pastor Cox was facing the door; he was getting off at her stop. Meghan's bruised heart was still weeping in her chest. She thought about Sophie. How confident Sophie had become. *"What had changed her so fast?"* Meghan thought to herself.

Meghan got up from her seat and stood next to Pastor Cox and waited as the train pulled into Franklin Ave. She could feel his intensity emitting from his body. She wanted to say something to him. She wanted to ask for help, or maybe she just needed someone to talk to.

As the train doors opened Pastor Cox looked at her. "If you need someone to talk to."

It was as if he had read her mind. She took the card he handed her. And *Bang*.

Meghan was spread eagle on her couch screaming for the good Lord Jesus while Pastor Cox plowed his way to a beautiful harvest. He was so deep in her pulpit that her ears popped. The back of his shirt was soaked; they were both fully dressed.

The most they had accomplished was sliding her underwear to the side and his dick out the zipper but that made it even more intense. Urgency and very intense sex go hand in hand like preachers and pulpits.

Chapter Thirty Nine

"What you doing here man?" Brenton was surprised to see KEV at Mo's.

It was early evening. Why was KEV here in the back of Mo's lounging? This was where folks came after work to grab a quick drink or a bite or to catch a game. This was definitely not a place that KEV would frequent.

"Just chillin, catching a drink with ah, what's her name, ah." KEV was having problems remembering her name.

"Marla?" Brenton was not surprised. "You are doing good for yourself," he said approvingly while nodding his head.

"You know." KEV shrugged.

Marla returned from the bathroom, she was shocked to see Brenton.

"Hey you." She tried to act normal.

"Hey, how are you?" Brenton pretended he was shocked.

"Not bad, still working on the piece about KEV." She looked at KEV for his agreement.

KEV wanted no part of it but he was too high to really care so he played along.

"Yeah, we here finishing up the interview."

"But I thought…" Brenton was about to blow their cover but he decided to hold it in. "You know what, let me get ya'll a drink, what you having?"

Brenton stood up to get his wallet. Marla's eye went straight to his crotch. And *Bang*. She had a flash of their first meeting. She sighed on the inside. In her head she was trying to figure out a way to shake KEV.

KEV wanted a Hennessey neat. Marla wanted a glass of white wine. Chardonnay. Before Brenton could get to the bar Marla had changed her mind so she trailed him to the bar.

"Can I get a Café Patron with a shot of Patron Silver, I'm trying to get in trouble tonight," she said flirtatiously as she slipped her finger down his chest.

Brenton felt a little bit of jealousy creep into his body. He did not really care much about Marla but the idea of KEV snatching a woman from him bothered him intensely.

Suddenly there was a commotion at the door. Brenton looked up; it was Daren, *"who else?"* he thought. Daren was like a walking storm.

"Lord." Brenton tried to be as invisible as he could, but there is no hiding from Daren.

"Hey Brenton," he shouted across the room in his very festive kind of way.

"What's up?" Brenton said as he approached.

He gave Brenton a full frontal hug. "Mmm, somebody smells good."

Daren surveyed the top shelf bottles.

"By the way this is my friend Tom, Tom this is Brenton."

"Nice to meet you." Brenton shook the young man's hand.

Tom had a Jerry Seinfeld head on the body of a twelve year old.

"Who is this hussy here?" Daren turned his attention to Marla.

"I am Marla." Marla looked him up and down and smiled.

Daren was pretty entertaining if you were allergic to his obnoxious nature. Marla was allergic to his obnoxious nature.

Daren flipped his imaginary hair to the back as he asked, "What are you having Tom?"

"Cider?" Tom replied

"Cider, eww, you and that damn cider?" Daren looked him up and down. "Sometimes I wonder about you."

"What's wrong with cider?" Tom poured on a dose of feisty.

Daren did his hold it together fingers, pursed his lips and ordered. "One grey goose with tonic and a cider," he said Cider with disgust in his voice. "I don't know who drinks cider."

He turned his eyes back to Tom. Brenton took his drinks and hurried off.

"We'll come find you." Daren hurried the statement out as Brenton and Marla walked off.

Within minutes Mo's was packed. The after work crowd was in full bloom. The low lights made for a very sexy atmosphere. The music was typical dive-bar music, not that Mo's was a dive-bar but they suffered from dive-bar music affliction.

Daren had squeezed Tom and himself into the cove of lounge seating that Brenton, KEV and Marla occupied. Daren had his legs crossed; crossing legs for Daren was like pulling off an extremely difficult yoga pose. Marla was highly amused by him. KEV was peeved to the point of almost punching Daren in the face. Why? Daren kept touching his thigh and rubbing his shoulder.

It was not that KEV was homophobic; it was just that Daren was so far over the line with his touches that KEV felt like he had to draw a line and that line was going to be in Daren's face.

"Ma man, don't fucking touch my thigh again a'ight." KEV went from Fort Greene chic to Bed-Stuy do or die at the drop of a dime.

"What?" Daren looked him up and down. "I don't know what you are talking about, ain't nobody want you."

Daren looked off into the distance. KEV gritted his teeth.

Brenton nudged KEV. "It's not worth it, trust me."

Brenton got the attention of one of the waitresses. He whispered something to her. She smiled. In a few minutes she returned with a tray filled with shots. KEV was happy again. Daren was all alight. Marla's dream was coming through. She was definitely getting laid tonight.

The night outside was shoved up against the window. The thick smell of summer was in everything. Brenton thought about Emily. The alcohol was speaking beautiful poems in his blood. Marla was sliding her hand gently along Brenton's thigh. KEV was a little upset but Brenton was family so he brushed it off. Daren and Tom were whispering to each other about some guy standing across the room.

KEV's phone rang. He looked at the number. He did not answer. He sat quiet for a few seconds.

"I gotta roll man," he said to Brenton as he stood up to leave. He was drunker than he thought.

Daren moved so he could leave.

"Where are you going?" Daren demanded.

KEV looked him in the eye. He thought for a few seconds.

"What, you want a ride?"

"Kind of, yes." Daren was flirting.

KEV narrowed his eyes and looked at Daren.

Brenton wanted to get rid of Daren. "Give him a ride man, you have to pass where he is staying, you at Maurice's right?"

Daren answered, "Yep, Washington and Myrtle."

KEV gave Brenton the evil eye.

Daren took that moment to further impose himself. "Can you drop Tom too."

Brenton looked a KEV and shrugged.

KEV hissed. "Fuck it, let's go."

Chapter Forty

It was about ten when KEV pulled up outside of Maurice's house on Washington in his white SUV, the windows tinted in a tight black, the vehicle nestled under a small oak tree in front of the house.

There was an awkward silence. Daren turned slightly in his seat partially facing KEV. KEV looked over at him.

"This is the place right?"

Daren answered, "Yes." Then smiled gently while rubbing his hand across the leather.

KEV took a deep breath, *"could this nigga just go already?"* he thought.

"So you gon' let me suck it or what?" Daren said.

KEV was so shocked by what he heard he did not know if he should get upset or if he should laugh. He closed his eyes and took another deep breath.

"What the fuck you just say nigga?" He was clearly upset.

Daren did not believe him for a second. "I'm just saying, I could suck it for like five minutes, that's all, five minutes, you can even come in my mouth if you want to." He gave KEV his seductive eyes. And *Bang*.

KEV looked at Daren and wondered, *"does this nigga know that I ...? No, no way, how could he?"* KEV was having a crisis, he was debating in his head whether Daren was a safe person to even have this kind of... *"Nah, this dude was too flamboyant, his business would be all over the place..."*

Maybe it was the alcohol in his blood, maybe it was the warm summer wind rustling through the leaves, maybe it was just the syrupy night all sticky with yearnings of summer, but somehow KEV was a little turned on. Daren saw it in his eyes, he licked his lips. KEV tightened his fist and grabbed the arm rest.

Daren looked at KEV in all his hip hop machismo and bravado and said in his deep baritone, "You know you want me to suck it, right."

He gave KEV his dagger through the heart eyes. That was it.

KEV raised his hand and gently grabbed the back of Daren's head. "Nigga if you ever..."

Daren slid his hand across KEV's thigh and grabbed his dick softly. The teeth of his zipper opened slowly.

KEV whipped his dick out. "You better not ever tell anybody about this shit."

KEV was as hard as a beam of steel. Daren clasped it with both hands and went to work. KEV

207

moaned as he stuffed his dick into Daren's mouth and pressed Daren's head into his lap.

Chapter Forty One

"So what's the deal with you and KEV?" Brenton asked smiling.

"Nothing, besides the article I am doing. I am a big fan, that's all." Marla knew she was lying.

Brenton knew she was lying also.

"Cool." Brenton shrugged one shoulder.

"What?" Marla felt unsure what his 'cool' meant.

"I was just hoping you would have told me the truth." Brenton did not really care what she did but to watch her sweat through this would be fun.

"I, I am just saying, you know, you don't get to meet one of your favorite artists every day, you know, and he's a nice guy."

Brenton smiled. "Marla I don't care, I swear, I know you fucked him and that's fine."

"I didn't, I did, I am so sorry, when I walked outside with him after that interview I totally did not want to go, but something kept telling me to go."

Marla was *white girl* drunk by this time. Brenton was *whatever bitch* drunk by this time. He did not care and she couldn't tell, so her apology turned into tears. There is nothing in the world that Brenton hated more than drunken tears. Why? Drunken tears are no fun.

"Listen, I am gonna get a cab and head home, ok." Brenton was making an unceremonious exit through the side door.

Marla followed behind him.

"Can you walk me to my door?" Marla looked pitiful.

Brenton's phone buzzed in his pocket. It was a text. It was Emily. *You should stop by.*

"I'll walk you to the door of your building," Brenton had other plans, "and that's it."

Marla was drunk but that did not mean she did not have plans too. She had planned to fuck Brenton all evening and nothing he could do or say was going to make her change her mind.

They stood in front of her building, Brenton looked at his watch.

"I gotta, get home."

"You should come up for a few seconds."

"Nope."

"I promise it will only be for a few seconds."

"You sure now?" Brenton asked.

"Yes I am sure." Marla smiled on the inside.

She was one step closer to her goal. Brenton's phone buzzed again. It was another text. It was from Emily.

"Guess what I am wearing?"

Brenton started typing while Marla held on to the door for dear life. The shots were whittling her senses away.

"I will be there in a few." Brenton texted back.

When Emily got the text she was laying on her back with two fingers in her mouth and the other two gently massaging her clit. The circular motions were audibly creamy; her fingers were sticky with juices. All she wanted now was for Brenton to ring her door bell. And just as she had the thought, her bell rang. It was Brenton. She opened the door. She was sad that he was drunk, happy he was hard as calculus. She shoved him onto her bed.

Marla was stumbling around her apartment trying to figure out what happened to Brenton. After a while she gave up. She stumbled to her panty drawer and took out a giant vibrator.

"See, you are here, we are going to have a little fun, ok." She was talking to the vibrator as if it was a real person. And *Bang*.

Chapter Forty Two

"And he is fine with you and me?" Brenton did not know how to process Emily's life.

"Yes, we have an open relationship," Emily said with so much ease.

"And he never gets jealous?" Brenton watched her closely.

"No, not that I know of." Emily smiled and cupped his face.

"I think he would be jealous of you though." She knew deep down that she was falling for Brenton but she had to keep her cool.

"And why is that?" Brenton kind of knew also that she was falling but he was also falling; he had to keep his cool.

Emily stared at his body, it was not perfect, but with a little work he could be beautiful. She passed her fingers gently across his chest. He took a breath.

"Because you are different."

Her words were barely audible but it did not matter because her fingers said all he needed to hear. She loved him and he knew it. The sun crept into the room and warmed their bodies. Emily snuggled up really close to Brenton.

"I think I'm gonna cancel all my clients today." She said in a dreamy voice.

"Why?" Brenton was never a proponent of not making money.

"Because I just want to lay here all day with you, maybe order in and we could," she put her mouth flush against his ear and whispered, "make love all day long."

Brenton felt a beautiful feeling pass through his body.

"Who are you?" He got up on one elbow and looked into her dark brown eyes.

"I'm Emily Dangerfield," she said with innocence.

"No not your name, I mean who are you?"

Brenton really wanted to know because he had never met a woman before who had ever kept his total undivided attention. There had to be something special about Emily. He wanted to know. She looked into his eyes and realized what he was asking.

"I am just a girl Brenton, a girl that thinks you are pretty neat." She snuggled up even closer.

Brenton was at peace. He had finally found… and he dare not even think the word. Love.

Emily thought about her boyfriend. Her relationship with him was fine. They got along perfectly well but their relationship was risk free.

They understood each other and they both understood the world. But Brenton. Brenton made her want to do something crazy. He was a body teaming with risk, and dangers and careless abandon. Just the way he looked at her. The way he wanted her was tangible.

They laid in the bed for hours and made all kinds of love.

"Do you think in a hundred years anyone would care that we existed?" Brenton said in a low voice while looking up at the ceiling.

"I am not sure but I know I will remember you?" Emily said; her voice crowded with longing.

Brenton's heart broke in his chest. That was the perfect answer. How did she know those were the perfect words to say? Brenton sat up on the side of the bed and held his head in his hands, this woman was really too much. It was as if she was slowly infecting him with feelings he had never felt before.

Chapter Forty Three

Brenton is gunning his red and white vintage '65 Chevy toward JFK. It's Friday evening and the sun is perfect in the sky. He has his shades on. In his mind he is thinking, *"this is gonna be one crazy weekend."*

The traffic seemed to give way for him. It was as if the entire world knew he was on his way to get his cousin Trace who he had not seen in about five years.

Brenton pulled up at the terminal just as Trace walked out the doors with a look of admiration on his face, as if the city was a beautiful woman he was checking out. This moment could not have been planned any better. Trace was the epitome of the black James Bond. Who else would be rocking a tailored suit with a crisp white shirt at the height of summer? Trace. Trace was the source of all of Brenton's cool. He was five years older than Brenton in age, but sometimes age can be misleading. If measured in experience and craft, women craft, life craft, Trace was about ten years his senior.

The world for Trace was effortless. He would wake up one day and say, *"you know what I wanna go live in Hong Kong."* And just like that he would be in Hong Kong as if he owned the place. Trace had always been like this.

"Trace." Brenton jumped out of his car with his arms wide.

"Brent, how you doing bruv." Trace turned up his British accent.

"Damn Brah, you still got it man." Brenton looked Trace up and down.

Trace smiled knowingly. They hugged again. Trace checked out Brenton's slight pouch.

"You've been working out I see."

They both laughed. Brenton grabbed one of Trace's bags.

Two beautiful British Airways flight attendants came gliding out of the terminal. They stopped next to Trace and Brenton. Trace gave Brenton the signal to play along. Brenton smiled. He knew Trace was up to no good. One minute in and he gets to see the master at work. Trace turned up his Brooklyn accent as he pointed at the two women.

"So let me see, you are Christine and you are Penelope right? No, that's the other way around, you're Penelope and you're Christine."

Brenton knew this trick. Always remember someone's name but never make it seem like you remembered their name in desperation.

"This is my cousin Brenton, he's the Mayor of Brooklyn," Trace said with confidence.

"Mayor? Brooklyn does not have a Mayor." Christine said in disagreement.

She was a smooth cocoa brown, with thin features and a well pronounced backside. Brenton took note.

"That's my point," Trace uttered smiling.

Brenton took Penelope's hand. "Nice to meet you Penelope."

Trace cleared his throat, which meant Penelope was off limits.

"And nice to meet you too Christine." Brenton locked in on her, and *Bang.*

They were all piled into Brenton's vintage Chevy barreling back to Brooklyn. Trace was in the back with Penelope with his right arm firmly placed on her thigh. Her uniform buttons were half done. Brenton was focused on the road; he could feel Christine's eyes digging into him. He thought about Emily. He thought about Emily. He thought about Emily. He looked over and Christine's eyes were so dreamy and wanting.

"So are we going to your place?" She bit the tip of her pinky finger.

Brenton glimpsed over his shoulder at Trace.

Trace shrugged. "Fuck it why not."

"How about we get these ladies a drink first?" Brenton suggested.

"What do you have in mind?" Penelope asked.

"There is this really nice Irish pub down the block from where I live."

"Anything will do, we are just here for tonight then we are headed back to London," Christine said with a certain amount of *I want you to fuck me please* hammered into her voice.

Brenton forgot about Emily. It was not that he did not care about her but he knew she had a boyfriend and he knew how he felt and maybe Christine could help him get some perspective.

And a whole lot of perspective she did give him. They slammed back a few shots at the Emerson before they headed back to Brenton's. His house was a pre party wreck. There were bottles of alcohol everywhere. Party groceries crowded around in odd groupings in the kitchen.

"So how are we going to do this?" Trace looked at both women in earnest.

"I'm staying with you." Penelope stuck her finger into Trace's chest.

Her slender English body was a graceful piece of art. Trace took her finger and placed it between his teeth. And led her by her finger to the bedroom he was staying in.

Christine looked at Brenton. "I guess this means..."

"We are here," Brenton said pointing at his bedroom door.

He could not have said it any sooner. Christine planted a tequila infused kiss flush on Brenton's lips. She was pretty tasty. Her English accent rolled around in his mouth.

She had been working on a flight all day and she wanted something firm to ease a little of the tension that was built up in her body. Brenton was more than happy to help her ease as much tension as she wanted.

He did not even take her uniform off. He reached up under her skirt and tore off her dark blue stocking. And *Bang*.

As he slowly pushed his way inside of her, his mind flashed on Emily. He felt a brutal sting. He felt like he was betraying her. *"What the fuck,"* he thought to himself. *"She has a boyfriend."*

He slowed his stroke but Christine was not going to have any part of this so she flipped him over hiked her skirt up around her waist and rode him until she was pleasantly satisfied.

Chapter Forty Four

Brenton's apartment was in a hush for a few hours. Brenton and Christine lay spent on his bed while Trace sat up in the other room clicking through cable channels and every so often taking a glimpse at Penelope's lovely milk white ass.

Trace was a little restless; he wanted to go see Brooklyn. He walked into the living room and sat on the couch in his boxers. The apartment was kind of warm so he wandered out onto the roof. The view of the city was breathtaking. All those lights, all those people just tumbling toward oblivion. Trace was pensive for a while. He was thinking about moving back to New York, Brooklyn felt right. Maybe later on or tomorrow he could build with Brenton about moving back.

"I'll probably get a crib like this," he thought to himself. He looked over the edge of the balcony. They were six floors up but the view was totally un-obscured. *"Fuck it, I wanna go party."* Maybe it was the spirit of Brooklyn that got into him but Trace was suddenly overjoyed.

He banged on Brenton's room door. Brenton jumped. Christine barely moved; she was wiped out. Brenton opened the door and peeked out through the slit.

"What's up?" His voice was groggy.

"Let's go party man." Trace had a look of excitement in his eye that immediately woke Brenton.

"Shit, let's roll negro." Brenton was game.

"What about, these chicks?" Trace made a questioning face.

"I don't know- what about them?"

"Did someone ask about me?" Christine was awake.

"No, not really," Brenton said in a quiet voice.

Christine sat up in the bed. Trace walked away slowly.

"Be ready in five."

Brenton slid his clothes on slowly.

"You going out to eat?"

"No, to party, I figured you were tired plus you gotta fly back to London tomorrow, right?"

"I am not flying the pilot is flying, I can party." Christine was wide awake now.

"Fuck it, get dressed."

If Christine was bad in her uniform she was down-right vicious in her normal clothes. She had a European/street style, kinda like she was from a gentrified neighborhood somewhere in Paris.

What was Brenton going to tell Trace? He walked out into the living room and there was Trace on the couch with Penelope waiting.

They hit the streets of Brooklyn like a photo shoot out of vogue magazine.

"Where you taking us," Trace inquired quietly.

Brenton's vintage Chevy crawled along Dekalb ave.

"Cafe Lafayette, we can get something lite, then we can head over to my boy Mike at the Brooklyn Moon for drinks, then we can go party."

The two women looked at each other, then said in unison, "We are down for whatever."

"This is gonna be a good night." Brenton could feel it in the sweet smelling moisture in the air.

Chapter Forty Five

They pulled up in front of cafe Lafayette and as soon as they pulled up, the car in the spot right in front pulled out.

"This will definitely be a good night," Brenton said again.

Cafe Lafayette was an extremely small cafe next door to Habana Outpost. If Habana Outpost was a basketball stadium, cafe Lafayette was a single hoop in a backyard. At full capacity the place could barely hold fifteen people. What it lacked in size it made up for in character and cuisine.

The food was impeccable. Penelope had escargot, trace had a Mediterranean platter, Brenton had a burger and Christine had a Panini. The wine also flowed. By ten they had forgotten that they were going to party.

They were beautifully inebriated when they stepped out in what was left of the heat. The streets were still a rumble. The crowd had spilled out of Habana and into the streets. This was usually when the cops would show up but tonight they must have all been on vacation.

"Let's go say what's up to Mike at the Moon."
The room was packed when they got there. This
was expected; after all it was Friday night. The air
was delicious with the smells piping out of the
kitchen. The only seats open were by the bar.

Penelope was a little upset. "Why didn't we eat
here?"

Brenton felt a little guilty. Why didn't they?

He just shrugged.

"Next time."

Everyone he made eye contact with gave him the
chin up or the nod. Yeah. They all knew what was
happening tomorrow; Brenton's roof top party.
Word of his party was everywhere among the
people in the know. This is why he was the Mayor
of Brooklyn.

Trace could feel the eyes on him when he walked
in. Christine and Penelope realized when they
walked in that they were on the pulse of Brooklyn
culture. Mike was behind the bar.

"Brenton." Mike reached out his fist to give
Brenton a pound while checking out Penelope and
Christine.

"Sup man, this my cousin Trace from London."

Being from London is worth a fortune in
Brooklyn. Yes, it is the accent. London might be
the only place in the world that gets respect from
Brooklynites. The room was filled with single
women on the pull, sitting in small platoons, and
Brooklyn women love men with English accents.

"Yes, fiyah." Mike gave Trace a pound.

"These are his friends from London, Penelope and Christine."

Penelope and Christine's top model status was downgraded to medium models status, the room was just one bad woman after the other. Trace and Brenton could not figure out why they were there with two women, but hey they were among the finest in the room so they were kind of ok with it. Mike was in his jovial mood.

"Have a drink on me man, for you and your friends from London. By the way, how is your boy Daren?"

Brenton was glad Mike decided to do this.

He patted Trace on the shoulder. "These drinks are dangerous."

Mike got an assortment of bottles and poured and stirred and poured and iced and mixed and shook and finally poured into five shot glasses.

"This one is called the London fog," his Barbadian accent came out.

The shot took them all through a small key hole. And after a few more drinks, it seemed as if time had stopped.

Chapter Forty Six

Brenton shouted into his phone as people milled by. He was standing on the sidewalk in front of Brooklyn Moon. Trace and the two girls were by the bar. It was a call from some random promoter in some random city maybe a lifetime away.

"Listen, I can't talk now, call me back in the morning."

The voice on the other end shouted back, "Brenton listen, the single is amazing. I am in a club and the single just played…, I can tell you this much, it is gonna be a Mega hit, I just want to lock down a few dates as soon as possible."

"Hold on," Brenton's voice trailed off.

It was Emily. His mouth dropped.

"What the fuck?" He did not know what else to say. "Listen man, I'll call you back tomorrow," he said robotically into the phone.

Emily was smiling as she approached. She was holding hands with what can only be described as a petit white man.

"Hey Brenton." She threw her arms around him. "This is Jonathan my boyfriend."

She spoke as if Brenton was not just inside of her a few hours ago. She spoke as if none of what happened between them was real. Brenton was hurt, hurt not by her being with her boyfriend, but by her indifference. This was the first time in his life he felt like he did not matter. He looked into the Brooklyn Moon. He saw Trace and the two women they came with. He finally understood how the women he ran through felt. His heart broke in his chest.

"We were gonna grab a drink, you should come have one with us," she flirted a little.

"I, I am with a few friends inside." Brenton was fully in shock; it felt like an out-of-body experience.

He followed them in. He introduced Trace to Emily. Emily introduced her boyfriend. Brenton introduced Penelope and Christine. Two shots later and they were all the best of friends.

"What are you guys doing after this?" Mike asked.

"We were just gonna go to Mo's, Hard Hittin Harry is playing tonight," Brenton stated.

"Hmmm, Mo's… It's gonna be packed in there tonight." Mike said jokingly.

"When is it never packed?" Brenton replied.

"Good point," Mike replied.

Jonathan was not a bad person to hang with; Brenton could see why Emily was with him. He was easy going. Brenton tried his hardest to act

like it was totally normal for this guy to be all over
Emily, but in truth she told him everything up front.

Chapter Forty Seven

They walked into Mo's with a verve to party. Trace ordered a round of drinks. They squeezed through the tight crowd as they pushed their way to the back onto the dance floor. Emily and Jonathan found a place to sit and watched as everyone else tried awkwardly to fall into the groove of the room. Brenton kept an eye on Emily. He wanted her so bad, wanted her even more now that he saw her with Jonathan.

In his mind he went back to both of them lying in bed. He could taste her scent in his nostrils. He retraced every inch of her body with his mind the way he had done with his tongue. The more he sipped from his drink the more he realized that he was in love with her. Christine kept being touchy feely, Brenton hated her for it, he wanted to get rid of her but he had to be nice. He knew she would be gone in the morning, maybe he would never see her again, but Emily, he wanted. He wanted to be with Emily forever.

He pulled Trace to the side. He tried his best to whisper, but the booming sound from the speakers, and the room soaking with lustful voices, forced him into a half shout. Trace could barely make out what he was saying. Brenton's eyes were peeled onto Emily as he spoke to Trace.

Emily felt his eyes. She was so turned on by his intensity that Jonathan vanished. It was just the two of them now. It was as if he was speaking into her ears. She had a quick flash of him slowly entering her, every muscle of his body fully engaged in the undertaking. She lost her breath.

"I have never been in love before man," Brenton slurred into Trace's ear.

"What?" Trace placed a finger into his ear closest to the speaker to hear Brenton better.

"I have never been in love before man. And the only woman I have ever been in love with is right there sitting with her boyfriend and there is nothing I can do to convince her she should leave him."

Trace just got pieces of what Brenton said but he fully understood what he meant. And in the midst of all this unholy gyrating, this unprincipled mania, this chaotic tumble of flesh against flesh, Trace looked at Emily and Jonathan and saw the look of wanting on Emily's face.

He held Brenton's face in both hands and looked him in the eyes. "She is yours bro, she-is-yours."

He was like a military man encouraging his troops to run into sure death. Brenton emptied his drink then walked across the room and took Emily by the hand and led her to the dance floor.

Jonathan did not say a word, he just watched as they embraced on the dance floor. And maybe it was the way Brenton held her, or maybe it was the way she fell into him, the way she surrendered to him; but something struck Jonathan inside and in the moment he knew he had lost Emily. Her body folded into Brenton in a way that only two people in blissful love can orchestrate.

Chapter Forty Eight

Jonathan walked outside of Mo's into the warm dreamy night like a lost ship at sea. The acoustics of his body clanged against the night. He gritted his teeth and inhaled the chaos of the world and wept silently.

Emily had forgotten that she and Jonathan had promised to love each other forever. Some kinds of love have an expiration date, even true love. Time sometimes burn us down to cinders and we can either cry out into the darkness of the world or we can walk away silently.

A new fire was ablaze in Emily's chest and loins. A new world was dawning in Brenton's head. Finally he was content.

Chapter Forty Nine

It was Saturday morning. Brooklyn was barely awake. The moods and feelings from all the parties were still walking around the deserted streets. Max and Sophie were in the back garden of Pillow having lunch. They knew the owners. They had been coming to Pillow for years. They knew it when it was at the other location, a block or two down; most of the other customers were new to the Pillow experience.

Eating at Pillow was like going over to a really good friend's house and having them make you a private brunch. Brunch patrons were the party heads. The clubbers. The one-hit-wonders: the, I bagged a girl last night and I have to do the honors of feeding her before we never see each other again. The one-night-standers: the, I met this guy and I am just being courteous and giving him a last meal before I cut him loose.

The back garden was full. The waiter was from the Caribbean, he had a lisp. It could have been his lisp, but God bless the owners of Pillow for making sure the mentally challenged are employed.

He flirted with Sophie. Sophie flirted back. The margaritas were extra strong and tasty. Nothing like a drink to get over a hangover.

"You know who I saw yesterday?" Max said while busying himself with his Panini.

"No, who?" Sophie was totally engrossed in her margarita.

"Meghan."

Max thought about the threesome they had with Meghan. He smiled.

"Really? I have not seen her in like a week, we kind of had a bad, you know?" Sophie gestured with her hand.

"Falling out." Max finished her sentence.

"Yeah."

Sophie was distracted by a young man who had just walked into the restaurant.

Max's back was facing the door so he could not see what she was seeing. Sophie eye fucked him the whole time it took him to get to the back garden. Their eyes were locked. The tension between them was like a thick dark fog. Max was too busy with his food to even notice.

"She was looking a little weird though."

Max was picturing Meghan in his head. He got a quick flash of Meghan with her face pressed into the pillow with her ass in the air.

"Weird? Weird how?" Sophie was barely engaged with Max.

The young man smiled at Sophie and sat down in a vacant chair across from his beautiful girlfriend.

"She looked like she was going to Church. I mean she had the whole prudish old woman thing going on too," Max laughed.

"Get out of here. Really?"

"Yeah it was kind of weird, because she did not even dress conservative for work, right?"

Meghan was notorious for her tight jeans. She was notorious for scandalous outfits, period. She had an amazing body and as far as she was concerned, better flaunt it while you had it. If she was not as bookish and smart as she was, most people would think she was a hoochie. But the moment she opened her mouth you knew she was closer to Albert Einstein in tights and red bottoms.

The young man looked over at Sophie. Sophie felt her panties moisten. It was as if they read each other's mind. He gently excused himself from his girlfriend and walked slowly to the bathroom.

"I have to go use the bathroom," Sophie said to Max who was focused on the second half of his Panini. And *Bang*.

Sophie had one leg clasped around the neck of the young man as he nibbled ferociously on her clit and gently licked her vagina. She grabbed a fist full of his hair as she came silently, with her other fist in the air as if she was holding back the Holy Ghost.

She took a few seconds to get herself together and walked out of the bathroom as if nothing had happened. She went back and sat down with her fiancé, Max, and finished her brunch.

Chapter Fifty

Max's phone buzzed in his pocket. He reached in gently. He intuitively knew who it was, Amanda.

The text simply said, *"See you tonight."*

Max was almost at his last straw. He tried to keep a smile on his face while on the inside he whispered, *"I am gonna kill this fuckin' bitch."*

His blood was on fire. He had to find a way to stop her. Sophie took his arm. She was still thinking about that sweet boy's lips. She wanted to see him again. She did not even know his name.

Chapter Fifty One

As soon as they entered their apartment Sophie's phone rang.

"Hey Meghan." Sophie was glad to hear her friend's voice.

"How are you Sophie?" Meghan sounded distant.

Sophie sat on the couch in the living room. Max saw that look on her face. And *Bang*. He knew exactly what she wanted.

"I am good." Sophie did not know what else to say. "So what have you been up to?" Sophie asked pensively.

"Not much, just taking care of myself, you know, taking care of my heart." Meghan was asking for help, but she was doing it in code.

She didn't know how to be honest with Sophie any more. She remembered what happened the last time she was honest with Sophie.

Max walked out of the Bedroom with his dick as hard as quantum physics. He was gently stroking it in his hand. Sophie eased out of her underwear and positioned herself on the couch.

"Ah Sophie, what are you doing this evening?" Meghan asked hoping Sophie would say nothing.

Max slid his glistening dick into Sophie gently. She gasped and flicked her pelvis, gyrating and clenching her muscles on the inside.

"Tonight is Brenton's big end of summer party, it is gonna be crazy, you should come."

Sophie was back to her old self. That one question brought her and Meghan to times in the past when they were like two peas in a pod.

"I was hoping you were free. I wanted to invite you to…" Meghan sounded disappointed.

Max gave Sophie a sudden quick deep thrust. It felt so good Sophie closed her eyes and inhaled deeply.

"Damn, I wish I could but you know this is always the best party of the summer." Sophie tried her best to feign disappointment, tried her best to hold in the passion she felt under every stroke.

Sure she wanted to go to whatever other thing Meghan wanted her to go to. They both knew she was faking it; Sophie was the best at faking it. Max plunged harder. She almost forgot that she was on the phone.

She looked at Max and mouthed, "Stop!" Then she smiled.

"Ok, then I was just calling to see how you were doing." Meghan had her tail between her legs.

"Meghan?" Sophie said quietly, "we should definitely hang out soon, ok."

239

"Ok," Meghan said before she hung up.

Chapter Fifty Two

When Trace woke up the two young ladies were gone. Brenton had spent the night with Emily. Brenton had forgotten all about his party. Love has a way of making everything in the world seem insignificant.

"Yow, Trace, did Penelope and Christine leave?"

"Yeah they left."

"Christine was not mad right?"

"Nah she was cool, she understood." There was a long pause. "Nah she was pissed bruv, you should have heard her when we got back here."

"Damn man, I didn't mean to do that to her."

Brenton honestly didn't want to hurt Christine but he had no choice given the situation.

"I spoke with her though man, no worries," Trace assured him.

"Ok, cool. I am about to go get my car from café Lafayette and head home."

"See you soon bruv."

Chapter Fifty Three

The weather was perfect outside. The sun fell below the horizon and Brooklyn was ready for the party everyone had been whispering about. Brenton moved his bed into the room Trace was staying in. Cleared out all the furniture from his living room and moved the couches into his bedroom. His bedroom was now the chill room. He installed a black light. The apartment was an enchanted forest.

People started trickling in at eight. By nine the place was at a nice medium. By ten people started flooding out onto the roof. There was someone on the grill. The smoke from the grill perfumed the air. There was a table filled with all kinds of bottles on the roof and another inside. The crowd swelled to a point where Brenton felt like he needed to call the cops to end the party.

DJ Jahmed was spinning. Everybody was dancing, sweating, drinking, screaming, singing at the top of their voices, throwing back shots. There was no discrimination. Everyone was dancing with whoever was open, no one cared. The place was manic, was crazy, it was total bedlam. The hot air climbed through the crowd and spoke to people's bodies. The bass from the speakers shook and vibrated against the walls and folks were grinding against each other even when grinding was not necessary.

By midnight the ballers started showing up. KEV came through with a gang of women. The party almost stopped when he walked in. But the intensity did not drop; the more people drank the harder they partied. Yes, people knew who he was. Yes, he was fashionably late. Yes, this is how ballers roll. But no one cared. He went straight to Brenton, they exchanged pleasantries. The DJ gave him a shout out the moment he walked in and the party moved into a ratchet phase. What is a party in Brooklyn without a little bit of ratchetry?

KEV decided to use the chill out room as VIP. Daren showed up at one in the morning with about ten super models. Where did he find ten super models? No one knew. He had about a dozen bottles of liquor in two large paper bags. The party had to stop when he entered. He made sure the party stopped. People started clapping when he dropped his bags and moved into the living room like a futuristic pimp.

KEV heard the commotion and came out to check what was happening. He opened the door, and *Bang.* He looked dead into Daren's eyes. Daren flicked his invisible hair and twirled around and headed for the roof deck. His entourage followed like a small security force.

Brenton surveyed the party from varying angles. He walked through the crowd having small conversations, shaking hands and hugging those sober enough to not be sloppy. When Emily got to the party, the rest of the party ceased to exist. Brenton was single minded around Emily. She was the only person in the world when he was with her. She knew this about him, she loved this about him.

Max and Sophie were on the dance floor slow grinding to a reggae song when Amanda snuck up behind Sophie and hugged her. The three of them danced until the song ended. Sophie could feel the sexual energy coming from Amanda. She kind of liked it. Sophie stopped dancing and placed Amanda's hand in Max's hand.

"Y'all should dance, let me watch y'all dance."

Sophie stood back and watched Amanda. Amanda's ass rotated slowly. Max hated how close Amanda had gotten to Sophie. She pressed her pelvis in against his dick. He could feel his dick getting hard.

Maurice saw Sophie standing, watching his wife dance with Max. Maurice took Sophie gently by the waist from behind. Sophie felt him pressed against her. Maurice was a little uncomfortable but Sophie relaxed against him so easily that he did not know what to think. She felt her alter ego forcing her way in.

"Meet me in the stairwell in like five minutes." Amanda whispered into Max's ear.

"Amanda, I am done playing games with you." Max tried his best to sound stern.

"You know you want this pussy." She looked up at him.

Maurice was in a zone. He closed his eyes and imagined himself fucking Sophie from behind. Sophie knew exactly what he was thinking. So she obliquely spread her legs and pointed her toes inward. She could feel his erection pressed all the way into her ass.

"Amanda, I think you are going to have to just tell Sophie and Maurice, I refuse to let you continue to control me like this."

The room was so crowded that within a few minutes Amanda and Max were almost on the opposite side of the room from Sophie and Maurice.

"Ok, ok, how about we make a deal," Amanda sounded desperate.

"A deal? What kind of deal?" Max was seeing a way out.

"I need you to fuck me one more time and I promise, that will be it."

Max looked down at Amanda. He narrowed his eyes and cocked his head.

"I swear on my mother's grave," Amanda assured him.

"Ok, five minutes. Meet you in the stairwell on the 4th floor."

Sophie pressed Maurice against the wall. Maurice stood still. She reached back slowly and passed her hand across his dick. She felt the tip.

"Sophie is going too far," he kept thinking to himself.

She was no longer Sophie. She was a person Maurice did not know.

"I want to take you into my mouth."

"What?" Maurice eased her off of his pelvis.

She turned and looked him in the eyes. He knew he wanted to but she was his best friend's fiancé.

In his mind he thought about it. *"Fuck Max. He was trying to help my wife divorce me. I should fuck the shit out of Sophie for that."* In theory it sounded good but in reality he knew he could not do it. If he did there was no way he was going to be able to look Max in the eyes.

"Let me feel that thick dick," Sophie whispered into his ear as she pressed into him.

Chapter Fifty Four

Amanda was on the 4th floor landing waiting for Max. She took the stairs down. Max was on the elevator. The elevator doors opened on the 4th floor. He opened the door leading to the stairs and there was Amanda smiling.

"I see you made it," she had a little sass in her voice.

"So you promise that this is the last time, right?" He was only inches away from her.

"Yes," she replied their lips almost touching.

"You sure now?" Max wanted to make sure.

"Just shut up and fuck me," she said as she yanked up her skin tight micro dress and turned around.

She had no underwear on. She held onto the railing and placed her right leg on the third step. And *Bang*.

Max slipped a condom on his dick and entered her with a vengeance. He was going to fuck her as best he could. And that he did. On the first stroke he slid his dick inside of her all the way, up to the hilt. Amanda moaned and looked back at Max. He grabbed her by the waist and proceeded to pound away, firmly but quietly.

Chapter Fifty Five

Maurice looked around the party; he did not see Max or Amanda. His intuition kicked in, and it all made sense to him, *"Max is fucking Amanda."*

He knew it in his gut. He hurried to the door. He looked at the elevator doors. His mind was racing. He looked to the left and saw the door leading to the stairwell.

Max was grunting his way to a spectacular climax. He came, she came and just like that he exited the stairwell.

Maurice heard the grunting. He was almost sure it was Max. He hurried down the stairs. Max was on the elevator back up to the party. Amanda was on her way to the first floor. Maurice got to the fourth floor; he could smell sex in the air. He pushed the door open. There was no available elevator on the fourth floor. He hurried back up the stairwell.

Max stepped out the elevator. He walked back into the party as soon as he got back and went straight to the dance floor. Sophie was pressed up against Trace. Max was pretty confident in his relationship with Sophie but Trace was not to be trusted. He knew of Trace's exploits so as fast as he could he separated Sophie from Trace.

Sophie was totally drunk. She was also horny. She wanted dick but Max was spent.

"I have to go to the bathroom," Sophie yelled in Max's ear.

"You want me to come?" Max yelled back.

"Yes, maybe you can help me stop this leak," Sophie said with a drunken smile on her face.

Max did not know what to do. The condom was still on his dick. He grabbed the tip of his dick through his pants and slid his dick out of the condom. He hurried through the crowd as fast as he could. He headed for the bathroom with Sophie trailing drunkenly behind him. He held onto the condom through his pants. As soon as he got into the bathroom he shut the door, unzipped his pants and folded the condom into a piece of toilet paper and dropped it into the garbage. Sophie knocked on the door gently.

Maurice came through the front door. The bathroom door was right next to the front door. Maurice saw Sophie entering the bathroom.

He grabbed her hand gently. "Where is Max?"

"Max?" Sophie enquired as if she had never heard the name before.

Max was washing his dick in the sink. Sophie could barely stand. She held on to the door knob.

"He is in the bathroom," Sophie said; inebriation swallowed her speech.

"Oh, ok," Maurice said surprised.

He thought to himself, *"Then who was in the stairwell with Amanda?"*

Max opened the door. He saw Sophie, he saw Maurice. Sophie stepped into the bathroom and clicked the light off. Maurice was lost in thought.

Chapter Fifty Six

There were a million small conversations happening on the roof deck. The sun was slowly pushing colors back into the sky. There were groups of people sitting on the floor in circles as if they were around invisible camp fires. Talking, sounding philosophical, but making very little sense. The table full of alcohol had been reduced to a table covered by a glass army. The grill was sitting lonely against the wall, caked over with grease and memories of burgers.

The DJ was playing chilled-out sunrise music and no one had a care in the world, until someone said, "We should go get sandwiches."

Money was collected, orders were taken, orders were mixed up and orders were confused, in this blind voyage to the twenty four hour Farmer in the Deli. The group of intrepid deli goers came back with enough sandwiches to feed a crowd of five thousand. Everyone ate, and laughed and chewed in slow motion and pretended to be sober as the morning yawned itself into existence.

There were bottles everywhere in the living room. The chill room was locked. The smell of weed came from below the door. Brenton banged on the door.

KEV shouted back, "Hold on, hold on."

Daren opened the door, and stood with one had akimbo. "Anybody wanna smoke? We got weed. Where did ya'll get food from?"

KEV came out of the chill room, with a spliff in his hand. He had the munchies. His zipper was undone. Nobody noticed. He got a sandwich and sat on the roof with a bunch of strangers and ate.

Chapter Fifty Seven

Trace sat outside with his back against the wall with two of Daren's model friends in awe of his accent. He was trying to explain the difference between loving someone and appreciating someone.

"To love someone is easy yeah, but to appreciate someone takes a little bit more. Appreciation takes love plus respect, plus gratitude, so I would not say I love you both, I would say I appreciate you both," Trace said looking into both their eyes.

They both swooned. Trace smiled. And *Bang*.

Chapter Fifty Eight

Max and Sophie were still in the bathroom. Max was sitting on the floor with his back against the tub, his head on fire, readying himself to face the aftermath of his confession. Alcohol and honesty are never friends.

Sophie was in shock. She was bent over the toilet dry heaving; the blue light of her phone turned them into two phantoms. Her text light was blinking. The message on the screen was from Meghan.

The message read, *"Hey Sophie, just wanted to let you know that tonight I got baptized. I wish you could have been there. Luv Meghan."*

Chapter Fifty Nine

Brenton and Emily were the only two people left dancing in the living room. It was as if they were dancing with the idea of each other rather than to the music. They were two light sources playfully circling each other. In their eyes everyone could see that they were in that new love-bubble. It was just the two of them. The world about them was silent and invisible.

Chapter Sixty

Maurice and Amanda stood against the railing on the rooftop looking out across the city. They had not seen a sunrise in years. This simple and beautiful act of nature spoke to both of them as they stood there. Amanda looked up at Maurice. Maurice looked around the roof at all the people sitting in their little private circles then he looked at Amanda. He and Amanda were in their own private circle. He took her hand. And *Bang*.

The sun tore through the horizon. It was morning in Brooklyn. Amanda looked at Maurice, and a shard of vengeance grated across the floor of her stomach.

"I fucked Max in the stairwell tonight."